URCHENT ISLAND

URCHENT ISLAND

Novel By J. Lynn

iUniverse, Inc.

New York Lincoln Shanghai

Urchent Island

iUniverse, Inc.

For information address:
iUniverse, Inc.
2021 Pine Lake Road, Suite 100
Lincoln, NE 68512
www.iuniverse.com

ISBN: 0-595-29585-1 (pbk)
ISBN: 0-595-66024-X (cloth)

Printed in the United States of America

For my husband, parents, sister, extended family, and friends.

With a very special thanks to the family members that read and edited my manuscript.

And in loving memory of Virginia, Laura, and Kitty.

CHAPTER 1

▼

Milo Snow, a photographer for a new magazine called the *Photo Journal*, was just boarding a plane to leave on a job assignment on a small island in the South Pacific. As he made his way onto the plane, he threw his carry-on bag above him in the stow-away cabinet, then found his seat, closed the shade over his window, and began to prepare for the plane to take off. 'I need a better job,' he thought, as the plane pulled off the runaway and began to climb toward the sky. His travel would be fifteen hours altogether, from leaving New York City to his layover in Los Angeles, the lengthy flight to the Hawaiian Islands, and then finally the charter to Urchent Island.

The job assignment was quite easy, but still, the mission made him a bit suspicious because it felt as though his boss, Swanson, was trying to keep him away from the office for a while. Things had not been good between them since the last magazine party held at his home a few months ago. Swanson had accused Milo of stealing money from his in-house vault and tried to press charges, but there was no apparent evidence that pointed toward him, so the charges were finally dropped. However, the incident broke the strong relationship between them, and from that point on, Milo knew he was treading on thin ice. The magazine really didn't need Milo because there were so many new interns cycling from season to season, that his job was just not as unique and valuable as it once was three years ago. Milo was not stupid. He knew what was going on, and could see that his days with this outfit were coming to an end. As he was thinking about this on the plane, he pulled out the *New York Times* and began looking at the classifieds for a new job with a different firm. There had to be somebody he could work for without getting arrested by his boss. After all, other people had jobs like that! He paged down column after column and couldn't find anything relevant to his needs, so he closed the paper and threw it on the floor in disgust.

Milo was a thirty-one year old bachelor, who lived in a small apartment in Queens, was extremely underweight for his height of five feet, ten inches, highly allergic to peanut butter and rag weed, and hadn't had a romantic relationship with a woman since he began his photography job at the firm. Dating was not a big priority in his life at the time, but he still flirted when he was near females and he was always looking for the perfect woman. Alcohol, smoking, and drugs were things he didn't do. Mainly because he saw no reason for hangovers, promoting lung cancer, or wanting to die early, at least not before he had turned thirty-five. At his age, he was in his prime and believed he was doing okay without the toxins in his body. He was upset at Swanson and with himself for staying with the job as long as he had, and found it hard to forget the time he almost went to jail for something he didn't even do. His co-workers seemed disinterested whether he was in his office or not. For the most part, his social life was a wreck and he couldn't understand why all this had happened to him, but figured this assignment was just what he needed to keep him sane.

Fifteen hours, three airlines, and many security scans later, Milo exited the last plane and was half blinded by the bright sunshine glaring down at him. He quickly found his sunglasses and put them on as he entered the airport building. The building was nice and cool and he had no trouble finding his luggage and buying a bag of chips from a vending machine on his way over to the car rental building. As he stood in the waiting line, he munched on his chips and took out his car reservation form to see which car he would be getting. The registration box stated a standard Jeep Wrangler. 'Good,' he thought, 'Perfect for driving around the small tropical island.'

"Next please," the lady behind the counter remarked.

"Reservation for Snow," Milo said.

"Snow in this heat? You've got to be kidding!" The same old jokes were always ready to brighten an already long day. In spite of her remark, the lady cheerfully clicked in the reservation number, but frowned at the screen then looked at Milo and told him all the Jeeps were reserved. Milo thought, 'Okay, I guess I could settle for something else.'

"All we have left are Mopeds right now." Milo scrunched his face up.

"A Moped? Honey, I am a photographer and I have a lot of equipment. A moped will not suit my needs. Where is your manager?" She pointed to a man standing behind her with his head glued to a computer screen. Milo walked around the counter and explained the problem.

The manager acted as though he didn't hear him at first and finally said, "If you wait a little while longer maybe we will find something else for you." Milo could feel his blood pressure rising and tried his best to keep his cool. He saw an empty chair behind him, sat down, threw his luggage down, and closed his eyes. Twenty minutes passed and a couple of other customers drove off in cars the agency claimed they didn't have, but finally the lady spoke his name so loudly that it jarred him and the customer beside him.

"You have the choice between an eight-passenger van or a two door Camaro. Which do you prefer?"

Before he answered he tried to picture which would be more adequate. Finally he said, "The Camaro will be fine." Okay, so it probably wasn't the best choice for his equipment, but at least he would have something fast and sporty to drive around the island. He started to sign his forms, but before he did he noticed he was being charged extra for the car. "What's this surcharge?" The lady explained it was more expensive to rent a sports car than a jeep, so he would have to pay the difference for the upgrade. Milo was not impressed, "This is nuts! I reserved a jeep, then you tell me you have none, and now you are making me pay extra for your mistake? This is an outrage!"

The lady handed him his key and said, "That's life!"

Milo signed his name on the form, grabbed the key, and left in a huff to pick up his car. He found his car and noticed that the back seat had basically no space for his equipment, so he had to cram it in the best he could without damaging it. 'And this was thirty-five bucks extra?' he thought to himself, shaking his head.

Urchent Island was not what he had imagined. He thought it would be the normal, "Hawaiian style" island, but it was a bit different. He noticed huge gardens everywhere he looked. Flowers and vegetables seemed to be the landscape, rather than just palm trees and beaches. The island was isolated, and there were more tropical birds and sea shells, than humans on it. Few actually lived on the island, but a fair number just came to explore and then leave. There was one dock and a huge ship that sailed once a month to this island and several others carrying in supplies. On the west point of the island there was a very small town. One restaurant, one motel, one small grocery store, a fish and bait shop, and a gas station, presumably to refill the rental cars. Along the sides of the road, fruit stands were everywhere selling that day's picking. He noticed that there were more white, Caucasian Americans on the island than natives. As a matter of fact, he wondered where they were all hiding. A few minutes later he drove past a small motel and saw a bright light blinking "No Vacancy!" He pulled out the reservation paper to make sure that wasn't his motel. Luckily, it wasn't.

A few minutes later, Milo pulled into the *Urchent Motel* parking lot, got out of his car, and walked into the office. A short old man smiled at him behind the desk. "Hi, I have a reservation, the name is Milo Snow."

The office manager was very friendly and said, "Yes, of course, Mr. Snow. You will be staying in one of our finest cabins. We are pretty booked up this week, so we are going to have to upgrade you from your suite to a full sized cabin. They are lovely and a little more expensive, but I'm sure you will enjoy it." Milo started to feel his blood pressure rise again.

"I expect there is a charge for this upgrade?" The manager nodded. Milo started to get feisty, "Let me explain something to you. I have been in the air for over fifteen hours, I just had a hell of a time at the car rental place and ended up paying an 'upgrade' charge because they couldn't fill my reservation, and now you don't have the room I reserved either? This is highway robbery!"

The manager tried to calm Milo down, and finally he negotiated with him. "Sir, I'm sorry for the inconvenience. Here is what we can do for you. I will give you our best cabin and only charge you half price for it. Does that suit you better?"

Milo still didn't look happy. He remarked "Fine," and signed the forms. The manager handed him a key with a bright yellow tag marked 10A. 'What a crappy place for a vacation paradise for a family,' he thought. His day was not going as well as he had planned and hoped that things would not get worse the longer he stayed on the island. From this point on, he didn't even want to think about that possibility.

Ten minutes later, he walked into his cabin. The cabin was larger than expected, but was decorated in poor taste. A 1950's style came to his mind and he was wondering if he could tolerate it. He noticed the bed was standing upright in a bookshelf nailed to a wall. The living room was furnished with a sofa, t.v., and one chair. The kitchen area included a fridge, microwave, and a breakfast nook. Beside the bedroom there was a small standard bathroom. As he looked around the cabin, he threw his equipment on the sofa, tried to ignore the squeaks and moans as he walked over the hardwood floorboards, and finally sat down on a wooden chair. He shook his head and screamed, "Why me?"

After he de-stressed a short while later, he decided he was ready to get a hot shower and then some food. His internal clock was out of whack. His watch said 4:30 p.m., but *Eastern Standard Time* was more like 12:30 a.m. so he was just going to roll with it until his body caught up. He took off his clothes and threw them on the floor. Then he got into the shower and pulled the knob marked "HOT." Nothing happened. Next he tried the knob for the cold water. Again nothing. Behind the shower stall there was a note with horrible handwriting stating, "**Shower doesn't work. Don't touch. Will be fixed in a few days. Sorry about the inconvience.**"

'Great!' he thought. 'No shower, no water, argh!' He put on a new set of clothes, headed out of the cabin, and decided to get something to eat from the local restaurant. It was going to be a long week. He could already feel it.

CHAPTER 2

▼

On the south point beach of the island, a motor boat pulled up to a make-shift dock and two men got out of the boat and began hauling crates from the back of the boat up to the shore. "Watch it, Simpson, that is fragile."

Simpson yelled back, "Shut up, I know." After twenty minutes, the men were exhausted from carrying the boxes up the beach and both fell into a sand dune to take a rest. "When is Jackson meeting us?" Simpson asked.

"Should be here very soon. We agreed they would find us and be here to watch us unload." A few minutes passed and the men heard a loud noise like squealing tires. Sure enough, Jackson and his bodyguards, Gibson and Troy, were heading their way in a jeep and slowed down to park. Simpson and his pal walked over to the parked jeep and shook hands with their partner.

"You got my stuff?" Jackson asked.

"Yes sir, everything is here and on time. Now where is our money?" Simpson stepped back as Gibson towered over him. Jackson smiled at Simpson, then turned his head and winked at his bodyguards as they began to twist on their silencer caps on their guns. Troy and Gibson each grabbed a man and took them behind a sand dune. The soft cough from the silenced guns didn't disturb the bird in the tree above as much as the bodies toppling onto the sand. The bodyguards buried the bodies in a sand dune. As Troy buried Simpson's body, he noticed a nice sized ring on his ring finger, so he sliced it off as a keep sake. Just as he was putting it into his sack Jackson yelled at him, dropped the finger, and it rolled under a big bush. "Let's go now or I will leave you here." Troy didn't have time to search for it, so he quickly ran back to the jeep. Jackson started the ignition and drove them over to the huge MAC truck sitting just behind the trees. He told Gibson and Troy to go load the crates. The bodyguards drove the truck down, jumped out and began hauling the crates into the truck. Finally, they put the last box in and then pulled down the door. Gibson pulled the truck back behind the trees while Troy smoothed the tracks out of the sand. Jackson lit a cigar and watched as the truck headed north. His cell phone vibrated in his pocket, "Yeah?"

A very dry and hostile voice asked, "Is it done?"

"Yes, all done"

"Good. Meet me at Hastings Way in a half an hour." Jackson hung up and smiled.

✳   ✳   ✳   ✳

Milo walked into the restaurant called the *Happy Clams* and waited for someone to seat him. A nice young woman came over to him and grabbed a menu. "Follow me," she said. Milo was enchanted by the sweetness of the woman's smile, her lustrous brown hair, caramel colored eyes, and very nice figure.

Milo asked, " What's your name?"

"Aerial, nice to meet you."

"Pleasure is all mine!" Milo replied as he grinned. She handed him a menu and walked away. Milo looked over the menu. He couldn't remember the last time he had eaten, so he figured he would start with an appetizer. To his surprise, there were none listed so he looked at the dinner entrees. The crab and lobster entree appealed to him. A minute later, Aerial reappeared and took his order. After she left the table, he wondered if he should ask her out. He pondered over the idea for a while and when she came over with his beverage he asked her if he could meet her after she finished her shift. Aerial wasn't quite sure about the strange tourist sitting at table nine, so she made up an excuse and told him it was too soon for that. Milo looked a bit disappointed but understood her hesitation. As a seasoned traveler, he didn't want or expect anything too serious because he was only supposed to be here for a few days. He knew the brush-off was second nature for a waitress, so he said to her, "I don't know anyone on this island and I was just wondering if you could tell me a little about the area. I'm a photographer, so I need to take pictures and then do a write up about it for my firm's magazine. If tonight doesn't suit, maybe tomorrow?"

Aerial breathed a sigh of relief. "Oh, you just wanted some expert knowledge. Well, I don't mind doing that tomorrow with you. I was getting mixed signals when you asked me out tonight. A lot of tourists seem to think I'm one of the attractions. Why don't you stop over here for breakfast tomorrow, and then after that I am free as a bird! Okay with you?"

Milo beamed. "Yes, that would be great!" His dinner arrived momentarily and he ate as though he had not eaten for a month.

After he finished eating, he paid his bill, left a generous tip for Aerial, and then walked back over to his cabin.

The sun was setting in the west and the tropical warm breeze began to cool down. He thought the island was cute, very isolated, but could be a good place for a relaxing vacation! He wished he had been there just for that, but the work must go on. Except for his magazine job, he would have never known this island existed. Before he headed back to the cabin, he stopped by the manager's office and inquired about his shower.

The manager, Otis, explained, "About three more days before the part comes in, sir, very sorry about the inconvenience. For the time being, there is a vacant cabin beside yours and you can use that shower until Wednesday. I will let you know it if is occupied before then, okay?" Milo nodded and headed back to his cabin. He rounded up his shampoo, a bar of soap, a towel, some fresh clothes, and headed over to the other cabin. Surprisingly, he noticed that the door was unlocked. Milo yelled, "Anyone here?" The lights were out and he didn't hear anything so he reached to turn the light switch on and just as he had found it, a heavy metal object met his head. Milo was knocked out cold. He had no idea that his body was being dragged along the floor or felt the tightness of the rope cutting off his circulation in his hands and feet that were being tied to a chair in a dark closet.

✳   ✳   ✳   ✳

Jackson's cell phone vibrated again. "Our men just arrived at Hastings Way. Where are you?"

"Coming sir. I was just informed about a small problem but it is being taken care of now as we speak. Sorry I'm late, but I'm on my way. Just a few more minutes, sir."

"Problem, Jackson? Please enlighten me." The voice became harsher this time.

"A tourist barged in on the cabin and my bodyguard had to temporarily knock him out."

"Jackson, this displeases me highly. Our plans cannot be altered. It is too late in the game for this to happen. I do not want this tourist killed because it will attract attention. You let him go when he wakes up and your man needs to apologize and explain that it was a mistake, not intentional. Make up something good. Understand me?"

"Yes, sir"

"Call your man, and get yourself over here NOW!" The phone call ended there and Jackson called his bodyguard to tell him the revised plan.

Minutes later, Jackson arrived at the meeting. They had just begun as he sat down. The head of the operation was a former army General named Frank Johnson, who had a passion for archeology and finding rare artifacts to add to his collection. The General made hundreds of thousands of dollars by selling these objects on the black market. While in Spain, he had confiscated an ancient map from the government because of its markings, and when he had translated it, he found it even more interesting. It contained an ancient legend about the Spanish gold that an old warrior chief once stole and hid on a small south pacific island. While the General was not one to fall for treasure maps, he was smart enough to recognize the real thing when he found it. He had learned a lot about the

Spanish government from classified information he would see from time to time. The map was the key to locating an underground chamber that interested him, so he learned as much as possible and then made his plans to find it.

According to one classified document, centuries ago the Spanish navy left Spain to explore various parts of the world, including this island. As they hiked around the north point of the island, near the Cynna Range Mountains, one of the men lost his footing and fell down to the bottom of a ridge, and landed with his face almost touching a trap door where only dirt should have been. Investigations led the explorers down a very long series of steps to a door they were unable to open at first. The explorers brought more of the army from the ship and they spent months figuring out how to get inside. Finally, they were able to solve the riddle, which was written in pictures and symbols, and entered through the door. Once inside, they realized it led to an ancient burial chamber that was sealed off from the outside world. A map was quickly drawn of what the chamber looked like as they examined it in detail. They noted the pictures of a sun, a crescent moon, and a pyramid on the walls of the burial chamber. After many attempts they learned that if they simultaneously pushed all the symbols into the walls, a second gated door would open. Inside this second chamber, they found the tomb of the great warrior SHAMBU, rare pottery, ancient documents, and artifacts. In front of the tomb there were seven questions engraved in rock. The inscriptions said that stones were to be placed in the hands of the great warrior. Each hand was marked either falsity or truth. They assumed that the hands would move to the next marking line for each question. According to the writing behind the tomb, it seemed that if all seven questions were answered correctly, the tomb would open so the keepers (long deceased) could clean the tomb and check on the gold entombed with the body. If not, the chamber would fill up with water and it would no longer be accessible. Since one wrong answer would prove fatal for anyone in the chamber, the men were not willing to take the chance, and instead just read the questions but did not answer them. Months later, after they had finished excavating and exploring the ancient city, the Spanish army loaded their ship with the items, recorded their findings, and found the ancient legend regarding the great warrior. This information, including the map, was taken back to Spain and put in the government's secret vault. At that time, certain officials of the government realized that this must be the same SHAMBU that had stolen the gold from a ship bound for the far east, and concluded that this island and probably the tomb were the hiding places of the lost gold. The officials tried to encourage the Spanish government to send an expedition to retrieve the gold from the island. However, due to the political environment at the time, the expedition never materialized. Instead, this was marked classified as top secret and only a small handful of officials knew about this island and the chamber underneath it.

The General had made a copy of the map and then placed it back where it was in the vault, so that it would not appear to be missing. A few weeks later he left Spain, charted a flight to Urchent Island, and carefully began to plan the operation. In the meantime, he hired ten ex-military men and found a partner to help him finance the project. It was time to give out the orders and let the operation begin. He would be expecting to meet his crew on the island and this was the day.

"Gentlemen, as you know, we are here today to begin one of the biggest explorations that we have ever been able to take on in this century. I hold in my hand the map of the ancient burial ground that has a secret chamber residing underneath a mountain ridge on the north point of this island. In this secret chamber, there is the tomb of SHAMBU, a warrior chief that once found millions in Spanish gold on a boat that was sailing east. The warrior actually stole this gold and for decades the Spanish commandos have been searching for it. However, today we have the map of where it is hiding. Gentlemen, we will find this Spanish gold and split it fairly. I will discuss the details of the map and mission later. Right now, I have put together a training exercise course for you and it will begin tomorrow at 0600 hours and will finish the following morning on the central part of the island. You all have twenty-four hours to prepare for the biggest expedition of your life. Are you ready?"

The men shouted in agreement, "Yes sir."

"Sleep well my apprentices. Morning comes early." The General lit his cigar and smiled, while Jackson just rolled his eyes.

CHAPTER 3

▼

Back at the supposedly "vacant" cabin, Milo had awakened. Just minutes before that, the bodyguard had untied him from the chair, moved him out of the closet, and placed him on the floor beside the door. His head hurt terribly and his vision was blurry. Milo whispered, "Hello?"

"Sir, I'm terribly sorry. I accidentally hit you. I was scared because I thought you were a burglar or something and my instincts took over my actions. Please forgive me." Milo looked up at the huge muscled man and wasn't quite sure if the man was really hunching over him or if he was dreaming this. He wondered what kind of burglar could frighten a giant like that? "Please let me take you back to your cabin so you can rest." The bodyguard helped Milo up, and slowly walked him out of the cabin. As Milo was passing through the main room, he noticed crates, a map laid out on a table, and two guns standing upright behind some furniture. Just then, Milo passed out. "Sir, Sir?" The bodyguard picked him up and carried him over to his cabin, and steadied him while he unlocked the door, then helped Milo to his couch. The bodyguard quickly left and hoped Milo would survive the evening.

The next morning, Milo slowly awakened. Sunshine streamed in through the big windows and blinded him. He managed to catch a glimpse of the clock displaying 10 A.M. At first it didn't register and then all of the sudden he remembered he was supposed to meet Aerial for breakfast. "Cripes!" he shouted. He had overslept and had a pounding headache. Quickly, he jumped up and threw on some new clothes and ran out of the cabin heading toward the restaurant. Just as he walked in, Aerial met him at the door with a frown. "Aerial, I am so sorry. Please, don't be upset. I had a really bad night and if you would give me a few minutes to explain about."

"No thanks," she interrupted his sentence as she pushed past him and walked outside. Milo tried to follow her, but she wanted no part of it so he backed off, cursed a bit, and then headed back to his cabin.

Milo sat on the chair in the main room and tried to clearly remember what had happened last night in the cabin beside him. He remembered going in and then getting hit, waking up for a short period of time, a man apologizing to him, spotting some things behind some furniture, and then waking up on his couch. 'What a bad way to start his day,' he thought as he rubbed his temples. All of the sudden, he heard a knock at his door. He hoped it was Aerial, but to his dismay it was just the office manager, Otis. "Hi yah! The part for the shower came in this morning so the repair man should fix it later today for you. Was your shower in the other cabin okay last night?" Milo shook his head and explained what had happened to him. Otis was appalled. "You mean, someone is living in my cabin? This is an outrage! I'm going over there right now." Otis bolted off the old worn out porch and ran over to the other cabin. Milo stayed behind rubbing his sore head. A moment later, the office manager reappeared by the front door and then walked back to his office. Milo wasn't sure what was going on so he decided to have a peek.

The door was once again unlocked so he opened it slowly looking for any motion. As he walked in, everything looked intact and the crates, maps, and guns were no longer there. 'Hmm,' he thought. This seemed kind of strange but he really didn't want to try and solve this little mystery since it really didn't concern him. Just then, Otis returned with the town's Sheriff and he asked Milo for a description of everything that had happened. Milo explained what he remembered and the Sheriff looked at his head wound, "You should probably get that looked at, so it doesn't get infected. Here is the address for the open med clinic." The Sheriff turned to the office manager and asked, "Otis, do you want to press charges here? Anything out of place or stolen?"

"Nothing seems to be out of place. Probably no charges pressed at this time, but I did notice that there were a lot of scratch marks left on the plate of the door lock. I will need to replace that."

"Okay, Otis." The Sheriff walked off and got into his car. Just as the Sheriff was pulling away from his space, the bodyguard put down his binoculars and called Jackson to report in.

*   *   *   *

By now, the men had been training for five full hours. An hour later, both bodyguards had arrived at the training area and began giving orders to the men. Jackson was there pacing back and forth watching the training, when his cell phone vibrated."Yeah?"

"Your tourist may cause us problems. This is your first warning." The call ended. "Dammit!" yelled Jackson. The one bodyguard looked at him and said nothing.

$$* \qquad * \qquad * \qquad *$$

Milo had decided to take the Sheriff's advice and get his head looked at. So, he asked the office manager for directions to the small doctor's office. He found the office without any trouble, walked in, and took a number from the counter. A large nurse held up a microphone and said, "Number eight please." Milo stood up and headed to the counter where she was sitting. "Injury, cold, flu, food poisoning, or other?" the nurse asked.

Milo replied, "Injury."

"Minor or major, sir?"

"Not sure." The nurse peered at him through her double thick glasses.

"Head, neck, arm, leg, chest, or foot?"

"Head."

"The doctor will see you in five minutes please take a seat." Milo had never experienced anything like that before and his head hurt even more just trying to think back to what all the nurse had asked him. He took a seat by the wall and closed his eyes. Five minutes later the nurse called number eight to follow her. He followed her back to the examination room. She did his vitals and then walked out. A few minutes passed and finally the doctor came in. "Hi number eight! What happened to your…just a second here….ah, yes, your head?"

"I had the bad misfortune of being mistaken for a burglar last night and someone hit me over the head with a heavy metal object."

The doctor examined the injury and thought his story was funny. Milo was not impressed.

"You are going to need some stitches for this. NURSE!" he shouted. Within a second, the nurse came in, nodded, left, and finally came back with a needle, some thread, scissors, a bandage, and a bib. The doctor put the bib on. Milo raised his eyebrows. "Just in case you happen to get nauseated. Sometimes feeling a needle pricking your tissue can have this effect." Milo rolled his eyes and passed out.

Twenty minutes had passed and Milo finally woke up from his dream. The doctor had already stitched his head up and he was laying on the examination table on his back. The nurse walked in and yelled, "Number eight is awake!" The doctor came quickly into the room and checked all his vitals.

"Hey doctor, am I going to be okay?"

"Yes son, you will be fine. Please come back in a week so I can see how your head is. Have a nice day and please pay on your way out." Milo slowly got up from the examination table and walked back to the front office.

"That will be $100.90 please."

"What? That is an outrage. For a few stitches?"

"Sir, your first visit you get a discount. Normally it is $50.00, but today you pay $25.00. There is an additional $10.00 charge for passing out without telling us first. The rest is for supplies, doctor's time, and my time. We take VISA or cash, no checks please." Milo dug out his wallet and handed the nurse his VISA card. The nurse processed it and handed him the receipt to sign. At least he could sign it off as a business expense somehow. He left the doctor's office and headed over to the *Happy Clams* restaurant for some lunch.

Milo walked in the door and followed another nice waitress to a table. A few minutes later, he ordered some water and a bowl of chowder. "Do you have a local paper anywhere?"

The waitress replied, "Over by the counter." Milo went over and paid for a paper, took it over to his table, and started reading it. The paper was quite thin, so it didn't take him very long to read the whole thing. The headlines were quite boring, "**Seagulls Nest At Southern Point Beach**," "**Local Mother Gives Birth To Twins**," "**Hastings Way Will Be Closed For Road Construction**." The waitress brought him his chowder and he began to dig in. He turned the paper over and noticed a very small blurb about two men spotted on the south point of the island and not returning to sea in their motor boat. The article ended with assurance that a further investigation would be done this week. Milo got goose bumps all of the sudden. He had hoped it wasn't one of the men in the cabin last night.

"More water, sweetie?"

"No thanks. Just the bill please." The waitress tore off the slip and handed it to him. He got up from his table, paid the bill, grabbed a toothpick, went outside of the restaurant, and rubbed his temples trying to figure out what he should do next.

*   *   *   *

Sheriff Thompson was making his daily rounds across the island. He saw a lot of wildlife, litter scattered all over a picnicking area, and the usual tourists hiking in different areas. The evening before, someone had called the dispatch service regarding the two men seen at the south point abandoning their boat, so the Sheriff was heading out that way to see what was going on. He arrived at the south point beach and started looking around. Behind the thick brush, Jackson watched him through his binoculars. He saw no boat, no men, and no trace of any footsteps, since the beach had been raked earlier that day. The warm sun made him sweat profusely so he headed over toward the shady area of the beach and took a rest. He wiped his face and took off his glasses. Just then his glasses fumbled out of his hands and they rolled under a large rooted bush. "Drat," he yapped. He was as blind as a bat without them, so he slowly bent down and tried to feel for them under the bush. Instead of plastic, he felt something really odd. It felt stone cold and very hard. He pulled it out and tried to examine what it was, but without his glasses he couldn't make it out, so he put it in his pocket and decided to look at it later. Just then his car radio started to make noise, so he quickly tried again to find his glasses and this time he reached them. He put them on and ran over to the car. "Sheriff, we need you at Hastings Way, there has been an accident. Please respond. Over."

"I'm on my way." The Sheriff started his engine and hit the sirens. He had a ways to drive, so he thought about the strange object he had picked up under the bush. He reached for a plastic bag beside him and laid it on his dash board. Just then his radio started to squawk.

"Sheriff?"

"Yes."

"The ambulance just arrived at the scene. Officer Garret is waiting for you."

"I'm going as fast as I can. I'll be there shortly." The Sheriff hung up his mike and mashed his pedal down. As he was passing the center of the island, he pulled the object out of his pocket and looked at it. He freaked out at the sight of the human finger and lost control of his car. Just then a car from behind him intentionally slammed into him. The Sheriff looked back to see what hit him, but just as he did, the rock wall in front of him stopped his car and his life. Jackson pulled away from the scene and sped down an abandon river trail. He stopped the car, got out, and pushed the car into the swampy water off the river trail. He punched the keys on his cell phone, yelled to Gibson on the other end, "Pick me up now!" ended the call, and finally lit up a cigarette. As Jackson stood beside a tree, little did he know that his back was facing a fishing pole sticking out of the river a few yards away. About ten minutes later, Gibson had picked him up and they headed for the east point of the island.

*   *   *   *

'Okay, okay,' Milo thought, 'It's time to do some work on this island.' He loaded up his car with all of his camera gear and stopped in the office to see the manager. "Is Otis here?"

"Nope, he is out fishing today. Can I help you?" Otis's wife, Lucy, asked.

"Yes, I need a map of this island please." She handed him a huge sized map of the small island and pointed out some spots that she thought would make great photos. Milo looked over the map and then asked Lucy, "How long have you lived on this island?"

"Let's see. About fifteen years I think."

"Any natives live here?"

"Years ago, a Spanish tribe lived here and populated most of the island. However, because it was a small tribe the families began to die out due to tuberculosis. It seemed that a Spanish fleet brought the infectious disease from Europe and once it arrived to the island the disease spread throughout the tribe. Very sad actually. For many years this island was unpopulated until the early fifties when a wealthy business tycoon from California decided he wanted to turn the island into an exotic vacation place for anyone that was willing to pay a nice fee to visit the island. These cabins and the *Happy Clams* restaurant were built for tourists to enjoy a nice stay and taste some fresh seafood. Over time, more people began to stay longer than just a week or two and soon, people like Otis and myself, made a life on this island together. We liked the idea of giving up the hustle and bustle of the mainland, especially New York City!" Milo grinned.

"Well, that does explain why I can't find any island natives."

"If you drive over to the east point of the island you may find one or two Spanish families living here, but us Caucasians are the majority!" He thanked her as she handed him a tour guide booklet and left the office. He walked back to his cabin, found his car keys, and unlocked his car door. As he sat in his car, he opened his guide book and read the "blurb" about the business tycoon finding the island, what he did, when he died, and noted that after his death in the late 70's he donated his wealth to the island. This of course meant that the one time fee to visit was no longer applicable. He started the car and decided that his first stop was going to be the center of the island where the wildlife was supposed to be magnificent, along with an ancient waterfall. He arrived at the area about thirty minutes later and found a nice place to park the car and set up his equipment. After he put together his camera accessories, he pulled his camera around his neck and began to hike into the wildlife preserve. Tropical birds and plants surrounded him. It was beautiful. He shot picture after picture of the landscape and wildlife. As he hiked further into the wooded area he approached the ancient waterfall and took more photos. He was quite happy with his pictures and thought that the waterfall would be a nice place to cool off and wash up a bit. Milo put his camera in its case and started to take off his shirt, socks, and shoes. He dove into the clear water and came jolting up. The water was quite cold, compared to his hot body, but boy did the fresh water feel good to him. He swam around in circles, peered at the small tropical fish and plants on the bottom, and then finally decided it was time to call it a day.

As he was getting out of the water, he thought he heard bushes rustling. He looked around but didn't see anyone, so he continued to walk up the rocks to where he had left his clothes and camera. After he finished putting his clothes on, he saw a beautiful fawn run across the trees behind the waterfall. He quickly grabbed his camera and started to put it together, but not in time to capture the fawn. Instead he captured something else. As he looked through his generic lense, he saw blurred images about a hundred yards away, so he quickly twisted on his telephoto lense and tried to make out the images. It looked like a group of men dressed in camouflage pants doing exercises. From his angle it looked like he was watching a military drill but yet there were no signs of U.S. Army insignia anywhere in the area. Milo thought this to be odd, but figured it was just something that people on this island did and he shouldn't stick his nose in where it didn't belong. For all he knew, they could be hunters getting in shape for their hunt! Before he put the camera around his neck, he decided to snap a few pictures just for something interesting to add to his island collections, and after that he headed back to his car. As he walked away from the waterfall, a bodyguard spotted him and watched him drive away in his Camaro.

Milo was feeling very refreshed as he drove back to town. He had photographed a lot of nice island pictures and was happy that he had actually accomplished something for the day. As he was driving down the road, he saw the Sheriff's mangled car protruding out of a rock wall. Milo didn't know what to do. He started hyperventilating until he grabbed a bag from the glove compartment and started to breathe into it. A minute or two went by before his breathing was back to normal. He quickly grabbed his cell phone and called 9-1-1. "Hello 9-1-1 dispatcher. Please state your emergency."

"Yes, this is Milo Snow. I'm on the highway between the *Happy Clams* restaurant and the center of the island. It looks like the Sheriff has been in a terrible accident. Please hurry with an ambulance."

"Sir, is the Sheriff unconscious?"

"I don't know, I haven't checked."

"Okay sir, help is on its way. Please wait there for further questioning."

"Okay." Milo pushed the end call button and took a deep breath. A little while later, a noisy ambulance and three police cars arrived at the scene. The EMT's jumped out of the ambulance and the officers got out of their cars and ran over to the Sheriff.

"Give the EMT's room, do not crowd them," Officer Hanson yelled at the men. As Milo watched this, another officer walked up to Milo's car and motioned for him to roll his window down.

"I'm Officer Watkins. Are you the witness that called this in?"

"Yes, officer, but I didn't see it happen." Milo replied nervously.

"I'm still going to ask you a few questions, just standard procedure here, but please answer them honestly because I do not have enough time to sit down in the interrogation room with you and give you a polygraph. Understand me?" Milo nodded in agreement. "Name for the record."

"Milo Snow."

"Where are you staying?"

"The *Urchent Hotel* in cabin 10A."

"Where were you coming from before you saw this accident?" Milo briefly explained his job assignment and what he did earlier. "When you came to the scene, did you get out of your car and touch anything?"

"No, I stayed inside and just called 9-1-1."

"Okay, how long will you be on the island?"

"Not really sure. I'm hoping to be here for a few more days, probably a week at the most."

"Until we investigate this site and rule out different things, I will probably need to contact you so I want you to tell me when you are leaving. Got it?"

"Yes, sir."

"You are free to go now, thank you for your help." Milo rolled up his window and the officer walked over to the EMT and watched as he zippered a body bag up with Sheriff Thompson inside it.

'What a tragedy,' Milo thought, 'He seemed like such a nice Sheriff.' Milo was slowly trying to de-stress as he headed toward town.

A half hour later, he arrived at his cabin. A repair truck was sitting beside his parking space. He walked in and found the plumber fixing the water pipes. "How's it going? I'm really glad you were able to fix this today."

"Yep, me too. One less thing on the list to accomplish for the week." Milo walked out to the main room and sat down on the couch. He decided to call the firm just to check in so they knew he really was on Urchent Island and not in Hawaii sipping a virgin pina colada. "Hi boss. It's Milo. I am settled on the island and I have begun my work today."

"Hey, are you calling me on a company phone? If you are I'm going to cut off your account."

"Well, yes this is the company phone, how else should I reach you?"

"Don't reach me unless it is an emergency. I'll have your ass in a sling if I have to pay for extra charges from that island. Now get your assignment done and get back here, you got me?"

"Yes, I'm trying…Hello? Hello?" Swanson had ended the call. "Bastard!" Milo screamed into the phone.

The repair man finally left the cabin, and Milo was ready for a hot shower before getting some dinner. Once again he did the same drill as the night before, but this time the warm water flowed over his body and he could finally relax. Things seemed to be going a lot better now and he hoped the worst was over.

CHAPTER 4

▼

"Just twelve more hours boys, and we will be ready to begin our expedition. I'm quite confident that you all have the essential survival needs for this job and after what I have seen today you all will be rewarded better than I had originally planned. Let me remind you, I do change my mind rather quickly and there is nothing EVER in writing because of that. So if today I up your share to twenty-five percent instead of fifteen percent, I may lower it tomorrow. You have to earn my support for yourselves. Okay, enough of that, let's get on with some strategy plans for tomorrow. By the way boys, this is a break for you so enjoy it while you can because we left the most challenging tasks for you tonight. Tomorrow morning at 0700 hours we will begin our expedition. We have a long hike to the mountain ridge and down the ancient stairwell to the chambers. According to the map, it is a two-thousand foot plunge into the dark, so make sure your lanterns and torches are well lit so you can see your way down the steps. If one person loses their means of light, then they will find their way out by themselves and no money will be shared with them. Okay, now then, at the bottom of the stairs we will find a door. We will all wait there until the following morning before we proceed. We're not going exploring while we're tired from the climb down, since that could cause us to make dumb mistakes. Please remember, every second down there is one more second closer to becoming wealthier." The men all smiled and looked at one another. The General continued, "Now, that I have your full attention, I will finish explaining our assignment. Once we are in the main chamber we must walk through the burial ground chamber and look for three symbols. The first will be a sign of a pyramid, the second will be a sun, and the third will be a crescent moon. I will count up to three and then three men by each symbol will press the symbol into the wall. This opens the gates to the secret chamber. Once past the gate, we will find the shrine of the great SHAMBU and begin our hunt for the gold. There will be seven questions to this second riddle and we will have to judge each one as true or false. We must get them all correct or the ancient city will fill up with water and we will drown. As a back up precaution, we will provide everyone with an oxygen tank just in case. Unfortunately, the troops that gathered this information for us failed to write down the questions, so we will have to work the answers out underground, but that is a small matter. After we get our gold, we will pack it up, and then rest in the chamber until the next morning to head back out. Once we make it back up to ground level, we will be transferred to the west point of the island to pick up our charter flight and then we will separate. Okay, any questions?"

The men in unison shouted the correct response, "No sir!" and then headed over to the next training field.

Jackson approached the podium and covered the microphone. "The sleeping gas has arrived, sir,"

"Good. Be sure to pack enough of it in your duffle bag for tomorrow. We will be needing it. And one more thing, don't screw up." Jackson frowned and walked off.

∗   ∗   ∗   ∗

Milo was ready for dinner; he was clean and smelling good. He had dressed and put on his favorite tie. He really wanted to see Aerial again. He walked over to the restaurant and peered in the window to see if she was there. Another waitress spotted him and said, "She is over at the dock waiting for you. Just a reminder, you have one more chance so don't blow it."

"I owe you one! Thanks!" Milo literally ran all the way over to the dock so he wouldn't disappoint her. There she was, wearing a bikini top with a matching skirt, looking incredible. Milo remarked, "Hi Aerial! You look amazing."

"Hi, stranger!"

"What do you say we start this over again. Hi, I'm Milo, it's nice to meet you."

"Hi Milo, it's nice to meet you."

"So, sorry about this morning, I…"

She put a finger over his lips and smiled. "I know what happened. This is a small town you know."

"I'm still sorry. Say, I'm starved. Know of a good place I could get some dinner?"

"You bet! Follow me." They walked away from the dock and headed down through a beachy area. Minutes later they approached Aerial's house. It was quite small, but looked well kept and her porch looked out to the ocean. She led Milo in and said, "I was expecting you." She sat him down at a table and there was a little place card with his name on it with a heart around it. "I hope you like pasta, because that is what you are getting!" Milo smiled. He felt like he was in a cozy warm home of his own and he never wanted to leave.

They finished dinner and talked about various subjects, but Milo didn't want to bring up the Sheriff's accident and ruin the mood of the evening, so he stuck to his story up to the accident. After she finished clearing the table they walked out on the beach and looked at the stars above them trying to make out the little dipper. "Thank you for a wonderful evening, Aerial. Sorry to cut it a little short here, but I need to call it a night. I hope you understand."

Aerial smiled, "Of course. I have to be up extra early tomorrow anyhow and a girl need's her beauty sleep." They both stared at each other's eyes for a few seconds and then separated.

*   *   *   *

It was 7 a.m. and Jackson, the bodyguards, and the ten men were ready and raring to go. "Good morning my little apprentices, so glad you are all here to experience this adventure. Let the expedition begin." BANG BANG BANG! The bodyguards shot three rounds off from their guns. "Hey, hey, that will attract unwanted attention you fools, don't ever do that again without asking me first, you got it?" The bodyguards frowned and dropped their heads. Jackson took away their guns.

*   *   *   *

The noise from the guns startled Milo and he jolted up from a very sound sleep. The noise must have ricocheted off of the mountain walls and out toward the town. 'What in sam hill was that?' he thought. He ran outside his cabin and saw a huge flock of tropical birds flying toward him as though they were flying away from something that had scared them violently. Milo was tempted to see where the noise had come from, but he didn't want to let his curiosity get the better of him. As he sat on the porch for a while, he started to think about the Sheriff's accident that he had witnessed. This island was beginning to be an adventure of its own, but he wasn't sure he liked that.

*   *   *   *

"The Sheriff was pronounced dead twelve hours ago. We have finished the autopsy and concluded that he died of a head injury from the impact of the windshield. His body will be here until funeral arrangements are made by his wife. Any other questions officer?"

"Not at this time, Dr. Coates, but thanks for your report and I will call you if I need anything more from you." Officer Watkins walked out of the morgue and pulled out his cell phone. He dialed the number of the forensics lab and asked to speak with Dr. Clyde Collins. "Clyde, Hi, Watkins here. Did your lab have a chance to examine the car and conclude how the accident happened?"

"Not quite yet, we are still working on it. Our team should be flying in this afternoon to begin the analysis. As you know, a small town like this doesn't usually need the whole team to be here, mainly because not much happens on this island."

"Okay, well try to get it done as soon as possible. This needs to be your number one priority."

"No problem." Watkins ended the call and pulled out a cigarette. "Bad day to stop smoking," he muttered as he snapped the cigarette in half and threw it on the ground.

*   *   *   *

Jackson stood under a large tree to take a short rest. The men had been hiking for almost four hours now and they were ready to relax under some shade and drink some water. "We are making excellent time men. After this short break, we will hike over that mountain wall and then we will be ready to find the secret entrance to the ancient chamber. This is a good day boys. Keep scratching my back and I will scratch yours with a golden glove." Jackson spit out some chew and looked annoyed. He still wasn't sure if his partner was going to screw him in the end anyhow. But just to be extra sure, he had brought his own back up weapon just in case and was determined to use it if needed.

The bodyguards came over to Jackson and asked for their guns back. Gibson spoke up, "We don't feel safe without them. I think it is in our best interest to be able to protect everyone if some unexpected event would take place." Jackson frowned.

"It's my best interest to not get killed by you two morons. Don't ask again." The bodyguards looked at each other and threw him an obscene gesture in stereo as they walked off. "Bastards!" Jackson yelled as he threw a canteen of water at their backs. The men slowly started to proceed toward the Cynna Ridge.

*   *   *   *

Milo decided to take a shower, shave, and get dressed so he could begin his day. He was a bit hungry so he went over to the small market and picked up an apple and a bagel with cream cheese and thought it would be nice to eat his breakfast on the dock. As he made his way down the main street toward the dock, he saw a small funeral procession passing him. The patrol cars and uniforms made him think it must be the Sheriff's wife and family in the head car. Milo felt bad for the family and thought maybe he should pay his respects, even though he had only met him for about ten minutes. On the way to the small chapel, he finished his apple and bagel. He used his handkerchief to clean the cream cheese off his fingers and then stuffed it back into his pocket. He found a seat in the back and watched as the funeral mass began. All of the police officers were present, friends, and other town people seemed to be huddled around the family. The mass was short, but very nice and Milo held a high respect for the priest in charge of it. As the processional with the casket started down the aisle, Milo's attention quickly went to the woman who was holding Mrs. Thompson's hand. It was Aerial. Milo was surprised, but didn't know how to react so he slid out of the pew and headed for the door. From the side of the chapel, where he was well hidden under some bushes, he watched Aerial and the Thompson family shake hands with people and then finally get into the car and follow the funeral procession down to the cemetery. He wondered what the relationship was between Aerial and the Sheriff. Milo headed back to his cabin. He felt for Aerial but wasn't sure if he should see her just yet, so he decided to get his camera gear and head toward the south point of the island to clear his mind.

*   *   *   *

Officer Samuel Watkins was now promoted to "active Sheriff" duty until the position was replaced from a transfer from the mainland. Watkins stood in front of the office marked, "Sheriff Thompson," and motioned for the officers to stand near him. "Men, I would like to make an announcement. We have lost a wonderful man on our force and no one can replace him, but we are going to have to keep running things as though nothing has changed. Our work is still highly important and until we get a new Sheriff on board, I'm going to be giving out the orders and answering questions when needed. Are we all in agreement?" The officers nodded. "Good. Now I need to see Detective Richardson in my temporary office. Everyone else back to work." Richardson followed Watkins into the office. "The forensics team is coming in this afternoon to look at the car and see if we can piece together what happened out there. A few things come to mind. First, there is the possibility that the car malfunctioned and he lost control, brakes went out or another car pushed him over, so first we will take that angle. If they don't find a faulty part on the car, then we are going to have to rule out accident and possibly consider a hit and run. If it comes to that, we have a problem. Up until his accident yesterday, I know that he was just making his usual rounds and that was the last I saw of him. There was an accident on Hastings Way, but the officers that called for him said he never made it because of his accident. I'm thinking foul play may be possible, but we just have to see. I hate it when I get these gut feelings. Sometimes they pan out and sometimes they don't."

Richardson finished taking his notes and rubbed his eyebrow. "Well, I will wait until you tell me what you want me to search for. I can make his rounds and see what I can come up with, but that's all we have to go on."

Watkins paced around his desk and handed him the Sheriff's log book. "By the way, Richardson, have you found anymore information regarding the two men that were seen on the south point of the island?"

"No, seems like a dead end. I took the statements from the witnesses that saw two men come on shore, but other than that I haven't been able to find anything else."

"For now, put that on the back burner. I doubt there is a connection there." Richardson got up from his chair, grabbed a map, and headed for his car.

* * * *

Milo was driving like a bandit across the central part of the island. He wanted to make good time while the sunlight was still shining from the east point of the island. As he sped past the forest area that he had seen the day before, a squad car was camouflaged by the fauna. The officer's siren came on behind him and Milo quickly slammed on his brakes to pull over. Officer Garret grabbed his note pad and walked over to Milo's window. He frowned when he saw the rental car sticker on the windshield and knew this was going to take more time than he had wanted. "License and registration please."

"I'm sorry officer, I was not paying attention to your road signs. Stupid me was trying to beat the sunlight to get good angles for the camera shots I wanted to take on the south point of the island. I'm at fault. Here are my papers."

The officer jotted down his information and wrote him a ticket. "Mr. Snow, this is a small island. It is not a big city where there are more cars than police patrols, where people get away with speeding and illegal road rage. My biggest pet peeve are you tourists that try to get away with things because you are on vacation. This is still a small part of the U.S. in the south pacific and we have the same kind of laws that you have in New York. Understand me?"

Milo nodded, "One thing officer, this morning I heard gun shots. I almost had a heart attack as I jolted out of a sound sleep."

The officer rubbed his temples. Tourists try every trick to get out of tickets. "Sir, I'm sure that you thought you heard gun shots, but there are a lot of other sounds it could have been. You are near the docks and sometimes boats make loud bangs as they slam into the dock station to get refueled."

"No, I know what a gun shot sounds like and I heard three of them. A huge flock of birds even came flying over my cabin from the direction of the gunshots."

The officer ripped off his ticket and said, "Fine. I want you to follow me to the station."

Milo was outraged, "Over a stupid speeding ticket? Why?"

"Because I said so. Now do it or I will put you behind bars."

"Fine!" Milo yelled. Officer Garret walked back to his car and pulled a U-turn, while he muttered "Dog-gone tourists" under his breath. Milo followed behind him equally peeved.

*   *   *   *

A few hours later, Jackson, the General, and the ten men were standing at the entrance way to the underground ancient chamber. "We're here! Now, according to the coordinates on this map, we should begin to dig down to the trap door. The stupid Spanish Army wanted to hide the trap door so they buried it with sand and dirt quite a ways under. At least they left the marker stones, so let's start digging!" The men grabbed their army shovels and began digging.

Jackson walked away from the commotion and lit a cigarette. The General came over to him and asked for his duffel bag. "No, not until this is done. I'm not handing it over to you."

The General got upset, "Listen here Jackson, this is my command and you will do what I say. Now hand it over or I'll have you shot."

"Okay, I will cooperate. Let me get it for you." Jackson started to pick the bag up and then decided that he was not going to be double crossed and threw it back down. As the General turned around and started to storm away, Jackson screwed on his silencer, then called to the General, "Who's in command now?" Just as the General started to turn his head, Jackson shot two rounds off into his body and the General dropped like a heavy brick.

*   *   *   *

By mid-afternoon, the forensic team landed on the island. Officer Watkins met the group and escorted them to the local lab. Dr. Collins greeted them inside the lab and gave them their orders.

"If you find anything, I want to be the first to know. Here is my pager number," Watkins said and left the lab. The mangled police car was still intact and sitting on a concrete floor in the basement of the lab. Dr. Collins began to put his latex gloves on and examine the back of the car. His team noted marks, tears, bent metal, blood, glass, cloth from the seats, and other miscellaneous things.

One of the field agents asked, "Dr. Collins, was the Sheriff missing a finger?"

Dr. Collins ran over to the field agent, "No, the report didn't specify that he had lost a finger. Let me see what you've found." The field agent held up a human finger with a ring on it with his tweezers. "That must be one cold ring!" Dr. Collins said jokingly. "Put it on ice, and let's see if we can get a fingerprint or a trace of blood for a DNA search."

Agent Jacobs, another field agent, took the finger and headed upstairs to begin his tests. Yet another field agent tapped Dr. Collins and said, "Dr. Collins, the back bumper has something lodged in it. I can't quite make it out. I'm thinking a shard of glass from a headlight or backup light maybe."

"Pull it out and see what it matches to. The backup lights are completely smashed out, so it could be from the backup lights, but I'm wondering how it would have gotten lodged if the glass had just fallen out and landed on the roadway. I need to see a picture of the accident site. Work on taking that glass out while I get the picture." Dr. Collins headed upstairs to his office to locate the picture. The two findings were puzzling, but the finger bothered him the most. He thought, 'Where is the hand that the finger belongs to?' He rummaged around his desk hunting for the picture. He finally found it and got out his huge magnifying glass. Sure enough, all of the backup light glass was laying on the road, but it was about ten feet or so from where the impact happened. That can't be right. He scratched his head. He thought to himself, 'The impact would have jolted the glass out of the backup lights and it should be right underneath the bumper. But it wasn't. This meant he lost his backup lights before the impact.' This did not make him a happy camper and this is why he wished that the police officers would have let him measure and take the pictures at the crime scene.

"Dr. Collins?"

"Yes."

"We were able to pull the dirty glass shard out. It is definitely not backup light glass."

"How can you be sure?"

"The actual backup light glass that the police picked up and put in this container have a different type of glass and lense. It is not the same glass that I'm holding here in my hand. This glass is thinner than the other and has a different type of marking on it than these other pieces. We also noticed it had a film of dirt on it, unlike the clean glass from the Sheriff's car. Sir, I think we have to rule out accidental death at this crime scene."

This evidence was not what Dr. Collins was expecting, and since he and Sheriff Thompson had been good friends, this was the last thing he wanted to hear. He never wanted to think that his accident was anything but accidental. After these new findings, he decided it was time to page Watkins.

At the police station, Watkins was sitting at his desk eating a sandwich. His pager started to beep and he glanced at the number. He picked up his phone and dialed Dr. Collins, "Yes, I got your page." Dr. Collins explained what the team had found. "I will be right over to the lab, thanks Clyde." Watkins hung up the phone, grabbed his coat, and headed toward the lab, which was two buildings from the station.

Dr. Collins walked down to the DNA testing lab and found Agent Jacobs. "Any luck with extracting a tissue sample from the finger?" Jacobs smiled, "Yes, I got a good scrape of dry blood from the finger and a perfect print, so I should have a match in about an hour for you." "Okay, good work. Page me the second you find out." Dr. Collins headed down to the basement and found Watkins talking to a field agent. He waved at Watkins and pointed to the steps to his office. Once Watkins made his way up to the office, the men sat down across from each other and began discussing the matter at hand. After extensive "what if's" and theories that seemed to be logical, they concluded that they needed more information on both their parts.

"Detective Richardson is out right now making Sheriff Thompson's rounds. If anyone will find something out of the ordinary it will be him. I'm expecting to hear back from him later today."

Dr. Collins sat back in his chair and frowned. "I don't like what the evidence is pointing to. Sheriff Thompson was a well liked man and I cannot understand why or who would have a motive to want him dead. According to what we have found today, someone purposely ran their car into the back of the Sheriff's and tried their best to run him off the road or into the rock wall and they seem to have won the fight. It's going to be very hard to find out who did this with all of the rental cars on this island. It's going to be like looking for a needle in a haystack."

Watkins stood up. "Not necessarily. If there is any damage done to any of the rental cars, my buddy at the garage handles them and he would not miss something like that. The rental place is extremely uptight about the smallest scratch on a bumper or a door. I will give him a call. So far you have found a piece of broken glass from a headlight, right?"

Dr. Collins nodded. "Glad to know that this rental place keeps a tight ship or we would have problems finding this car."

"Okay, Clyde, you find out who the finger belongs to and I'll try to find a body for you and who was driving that car on the island yesterday. Thanks for your help so far. I'll keep you posted."

"Likewise."

Watkins left the lab office and walked back to the police station. He wiped his brow while he watched Officer Garret pull into the parking lot with another vehicle following behind his. Watkins muttered to himself, "Great. Another traffic violation today."

CHAPTER 5

▼

Officer Garret asked Milo to follow him into the police station. Milo did as he was told and was shown to the interrogation room. This was not what Milo wanted to do today. Instead, he was being forced to sit in a boxy room with a huge mirror for men to watch him from behind and decide if he was sane or not. He had seen the movie, *The Rock*, twice and knew what went on behind the fake mirror. He sat at a small table and waited for someone to come in and get this over with.

About fifteen minutes later, Officer Watkins walked in and identified himself. He sat across from Milo and started to ask him some questions. "Officer Garret has briefed me on what all happened this afternoon. We're not here to discuss your speeding ticket, that is a different matter and you will pay it before you leave this station today, understand?" Milo nodded. "What we are going to discuss is what you said about hearing gun shots this morning. This is a serious accusation and not the kind of event that makes me comfortable. I want you to tell me the exact time and place of where and what you heard this morning. Details are very important to me. I hope we understand each other. Now go ahead with your story."

Milo explained everything that he could remember in full detail. Watkins wrote down what Milo said and then stood up to stretch for a minute. "Mr. Snow, yesterday you witnessed a tragic event with our Sheriff and this morning you heard gun shots. Is there anything else on this island that you have seen or heard that has been peculiar?"

Milo thought about the question for a minute. He finally started to speak just as Watkin's pager went off. Watkins looked at Milo, rubbed his temples, and then said, "Mr. Snow you're free to leave now. I've asked you enough questions for the day, so please pay your ticket and drive responsibly. If I need any more information, I will be in touch." Milo walked out of the interrogation room, found the front desk to pay his ticket, and then left the station. Watkins called a special meeting in his office, making sure that all the blinds were closed and the office door was locked. He unlatched the "fire exit" door behind his desk and waited for his special project team.

*   *   *   *

Detective Richardson had made almost all of Sheriff Thompson's usual rounds, except for the south point of the island, which was the furthest that he had listed last on his notepad. Luckily, the log book from the Sheriff survived the crash and they were able to find where the Sheriff had been the day before. The center of the island seemed very peaceful, the east point seemed normal and quiet, and at each stop so far he had walked around the area and looked for anything that seemed out of place. By the middle of the afternoon, he headed to the south point beach. He pulled his car up to the beach and got out. He noted that the beach had been raked, but there were some visible footprints above the beach near the brush area. He walked over to take a closer look. One set of footprints headed over to a shade tree and bush. The ground was moist, not as sandy as below, and kept good impressions. The detective measured the size of the footprints and double checked the Sheriff's foot size on the copy he had of the autopsy report. The prints measured a size ten and sure enough that matched. Before he touched anything more he paged Dr. Collins and the forensic team. A minute or so later, his cell phone rang.

"Dr. Collins returning your page."

"Yes, this is Detective Richardson. I need you and your team out here at the south point beach pronto. I found footprints possibly matching the Sheriff's by a shade tree. We need this analyzed immediately."

"We can be there within an hour."

"Good. Meet you here." The detective ended the call and put his cell phone back in his pocket. He walked behind the brushy area to see if there was anything else that he could find. Nothing seemed out of the ordinary, until he walked about fifty yards due north from the shady tree and noticed that some of the limbs had been broken off from a tree. No footprints, but definitely something had brushed up against the tree and caused the limbs to break. He picked one up with his tweezers and examined the somewhat fresh break. It was too high for an animal, but standing at this level, it was the right size for a human's arm or shoulder to brush past and break the small limbs. The detective thought a moment where that person would be standing in relation to the Sheriff if they saw him. He stood behind the tree and brush and noted it was easy to not be seen with all of the branches and leafy limbs around him. Fifty yards was just far enough that you could use binoculars to see someone and that would have been where the Sheriff had been standing yesterday morning. He continued walking farther back into the brush until he came across a grassy field and a small dirt road that headed in the direction of the main highway. Since the detective was still fairly new to the island, he had not explored all of the little back roads and trails that the island had. He decided it was time to do so, because it would obviously make his job a lot easier.

The detective pulled out his cell phone again and paged Watkins this time. Watkins was briefing his team when he got his page. "Should be detective Richardson. Hang on boys." A few seconds later the phone rang, "Richardson, what's the latest?" The detective explained what he had found and asked for a map of the island. "I'm not familiar myself with that dirt road heading out toward the main highway. Let me check it out." Watkins put him on hold and ran down to the front desk to find a map of the area. "Okay Richardson, give me the exact location."

"About two-hundred yards due north from the south point beach." Watkins looked over the region and found no road marked on the map, just a wooded area.

"The map shows no road. I will be out as soon as I can. Tell Clyde to wait for me out there, I want his latest updates."

"Speaking of that, what has he found?" Watkins explained what the forensic team had discovered. "While you are out there by the beach, just double check the area for a possible hidden body. That finger belongs to someone."

"Will do."

Watkins hung the phone up and continued his meeting.

Richardson put his phone in his pocket and decided to walk the dirt road and check out where it led. The road curved around just like he thought and did in fact join up with the main highway. However, he noticed the dirt road changed into gravel and a wall of brush that you had to drive over in order to meet the main road. The gravel made it look as though there was no road behind the brush. He thought to himself, 'What a sneaky back road. Only a criminal mind would have thought of a scheme like this.' Richardson felt a chill go through him. This kind of thing scared the crap out of him. He walked back the dirt road and came back to the grassy field. It was very open, but something that he hadn't spotted before he saw this time. He noticed another set of tire tracks had forced a path through the grass and it headed due north once again. Richardson wondered why everything was pointing toward the north? He followed the outline until he found another gravel road that met up to the field. "Where did this go to?" he muttered to himself. All of the sudden, it was clear what had made the path. It was none other, but a large abandoned MAC truck sitting in the brush off of the gravel road. Richardson grabbed his cell phone and called Watkins.

*   *   *   *

Jackson walked out of the brush with his bodyguards. "Attention men, change of command and plans will now be addressed. The General has taken a leave of absence. He was paged by someone that needed him to be elsewhere at this time, so he asked that I take over the operation until he contacts me." 'From the spirit world,' he thought. "We will follow his original plan and begin down to the chambers after you finish shoveling the sand. At ease." The men continued shoveling the sand and dirt. "Troy get over here," Jackson called. "Go over that way and bury the body, I don't want it to ever be found. Understand me?"

Troy nodded and ran over toward the brush. Jackson grabbed the General's coat from the make shift table and took the map out of the pocket. He laid it flat and looked it over, trying his best to familiarize himself with the geographical features. Jackson rubbed his temples and lit a cigarette. The map just looked too simple to be real. 'What was the catch,' he wondered.

*　　*　　*　　*

Milo decided to call it a day and headed back to his cabin for some peace. His day had not started well and it wasn't ending well either. He unloaded his car, unlocked his cabin, and sat down on the sofa in the main room. The day itself stressed him out so badly that all he wanted to do was take a nap and start over, so that's what he did.

A bit later, Milo woke up and felt a lot better. He was no longer stressed and felt very well rested. The sun was starting to slowly set and he realized how hungry he was, since he had only had an apple and a bagel for breakfast. He decided to stay in his cabin and eat something he had packed inside his duffle bag. He found a granola bar, some crackers, a bag of chips, and a can of soda. Maybe it wasn't a full meal, but it would be enough to keep him satisfied until the next morning. He turned his cell phone on and saw that Swanson had left him a message, but decided the way his day had gone he didn't even want to deal with it. So he shut it off and turned on his small t.v. instead.

*   *   *   *

Dr. Collins and the forensic team arrived at the south point beach and waited for detective Richardson. In the meantime, Richardson was talking to Watkins on the phone as he was investigating the MAC truck.

"License plate number?"

"MT 9029."

"Don't touch it, we will need to get the team out to dust it. Meet me at the south point beach I'm leaving now." Watkins hung up and concluded his "closed" meeting with his team.

Richardson quickly ran back to the south point beach and found Dr. Collins and the team working on the footprints. "Sorry I wasn't here when you got here. I have been finding more and more things as I have been walking around this area. I need some of your team to follow me." Richardson wiped his sweaty face with his handkerchief. "There is an abandon MAC truck parked on a gravel road I need it dusted and looked over. On the way I will show you a tree with limbs that have been broken, so please bag them and check for clothing fibers."

Just then Dr. Collin's cell phone rang. "Sir, Agent Jacobs here. I found a match on the print. The guy's name is Tyler Simpson, date of birth 1952. Last picture they have of him is when he was young and thin in the army corps. The FBI records indicate that the guy has been dead since 1970. Appears he was listed as missing in action in Vietnam. Not sure what his finger is doing on this island, but that's the best I can come up with so far."

Dr. Collins thought for a second and then replied, "Hmm. This makes it complicated. Call Agent Wellington and explain the case we are working on. Ask him for all information regarding this guy and tell him I asked you to call. Please have him fax all information to our lab."

"Okay, will do," replied Jacobs.

Dr. Collins ended the call and put his cell phone away. He and Richardson walked over to the MAC truck and watched the team begin investigating. They opened the back of the truck with a crow bar and found empty crates, three oxygen tanks, plastic bags, a tent, some sleeping bags, a grocery bag filled with canned goods, a cooler, and two huge tarps. The items seemed interesting for an abandon truck. "Okay, obviously someone has been living in the truck based on the food and sleeping bags. Not sure what the crates and the oxygen tanks would be for. Possibly diving?" Watkins lifted the crate up. In small print, the words said, "Tropical Fruit U.S.A."

"Fruit boxes? They seem kind of out of place since the island is full of fruit. Why import fruit?" Watkins was not liking what he had seen.

A field agent urgently tapped Dr. Collin's shoulder. "Sir, we found blood on the passenger seat."

"Okay, swab it and we'll get it back to the lab as soon as possible. Good work! Any prints?"

"Yes, lots. We have dusted them and should be finished soon."

"Also, dust these crates and other items in here. I want to make sure that they are all from the same person." The field agent nodded and grabbed her tool box.

Watkins and Richardson walked over and opened the doors into the cab. "The air isn't stale. Looks like the truck has been used recently and the gas tank is three quarters full." Richardson opened the glove compartment. A pack of cigarettes fell out, a jack knife, flashlight, and a contract that said, "*Anderson Trucking Company.*" Richardson opened the contract and noticed two signatures that looked like an ink spill were scribbled at the bottom of the paper.

Richardson handed the contract to Dr. Collins, "This should be some fun reading for your team!"

Dr. Collins studied the paper and replied, "We are fortunate to have a handwriting specialist on our team." Dr. Collins called softly for field agent Mahoney.

"Sir?"

"I need you to decipher this as soon as you can. We are most interested in the names of these two signatures at the bottom." Mahoney took the contract and looked it over. Watkins grabbed his cell phone. "I need to call Anderson Trucking and find out the deal on the truck." He dialed the number and asked for Mr. Anderson.

"Anderson speaking."

"This is Officer Watkins. I need some information about one of your MAC trucks."

"That's confidential, but if it is a police matter we can help." "I assure you it is."

"What do you need?"

Watkins explained what they had found. "I mainly need the name and descriptions of who rented this particular truck from you. We found your contract in the glove compartment."

"Let me check the records here. I will need the receipt number at the top of the contract." Watkins grabbed the contract from Mahoney and read the number. Anderson paused for a minute and then shuffled through his records.

"Okay, here we go. Two men from a mainland construction job needed to rent a truck to haul dirt. Names were T. Jones and G. Kelly. I hope this helps."

"Hold on a minute." Watkins thought for a minute and asked, "Do you have any identification from them?"

"Yes, copies of their licenses."

"I need you to fax them to the station. I need to see the faces."

"They are temporary only, no pictures."

"That figures."

"I have fingerprints though."

"You actually finger print your drivers?"

"Accident insurance, just in case."

"Cripes, what next? Thanks." Watkins hung up. "Anderson is a genius! He actually takes finger prints for his accident insurance claims."

Richardson shook his head, "The sun is setting. We need to finish up here as soon as possible." Watkins waived at Mahoney and waited for him to walk over to him. He told him not to bother to decipher the signatures any further.

The men and field agents headed back to the south point beach and began packing up their tools. "Clyde, tell your team I want to make an announcement." Dr. Collins did as he asked. Watkins stood up on a large rock. "People, this case is turning out to be something bigger than I could have imagined. Each hour more and more information is being overturned and I don't like what it is leading to. Here is what we have so far, but don't quote me because things seem to be changing. First off, the Sheriff's accident has now been categorized as intentional, so we assume he was murdered. We have evidence showing that his car was rammed from behind and the rock wall stopped his car. So, this is a serious hit and run. At this time we have no car or suspect. In addition, we found a severed ring finger. The prints match a guy named Simpson who seems to have been missing in action since 1970, but we don't have a body yet. We have back tracked and found that the Sheriff made his usual rounds out here and took a short breather by the shade tree. However, we don't know why he did that then, and may never know, but his footprints show that he was here. About fifty yards away there is a tree with broken limbs on it, as though someone ran past it in a hurry. One guess is that his murderer was standing there watching him and then ran to his own car by this brush in time to meet the Sheriff's car out on the main highway. It's a stretch, but we know someone was there because a car made tracks to the highway, and the Sheriff is dead. Detective Richardson found a dirt road that connects to the main road that the person could have used. And lastly, we have an abandoned MAC truck sitting about five-hundred yards away from this beach with empty fruit crates, a tent, sleeping bags, oxygen tanks, and the truck seems to have been rented by two men from the mainland. The puzzling evidence just keeps stacking up, but we still don't have a body to match the finger or even any live suspects. This island is small and it should not be that hard to find someone who sneaks around killing our Sheriff and who knows who else. Also, remember that dead bodies always have a way of turning up, so keep on searching for the possibilities. The minute anyone has any new information, I want to know about it immediately. Something is going on here and I have a gut feeling this is just the beginning." The team all nodded in agreement. The sun was just about to set so they all left the south point beach and headed back to town.

Before Watkins left, he asked Richardson a favor. "Has your job entailed surveillance?"

"Yes, why?"

"I think it would be wise for you to stay out here tonight and watch that truck. I have a feeling these men may have some answers for us." Richardson nodded in agreement.

*   *   *   *

On the north point of the island, Jackson, Troy, Gibson, and the men were ready to take the plunge down below. It had taken an extra hour to find the trap door even with the markers, but the three foot hole was finally dug and the bodyguards were able to pull back the secret trap door to enter the long steep stairs. Jackson and the men lit their lanterns and began the two-thousand foot plunge into darkness. Based on the altitude of the climb, Jackson estimated a time of two full hours with breaks before they would find the bottom. The expedition had now officially begun and it was just a matter of time before Jackson would be holding his gold. Troy and Gibson would stand guard at the top and wait for the crew to emerge two days later. As the last man went down through the hole, the bodyguards closed the trap door partially and then spread brush over the huge hole to camouflage it. Gibson and Troy hiked down a hidden back road and found the jeep that they had stashed behind a large grove of bamboo the day before. Gibson used the shore road to take Troy down to the south part of the island to get the MAC truck.

*   *   *   *

Watkins and Dr. Collins walked into the temporary Sheriff's office and sat down across from each other. "I'm going to order some take out food from the restaurant. You want anything?" Watkins asked Clyde.

"No thanks."

Watkins called out to the staff assistant and asked her to place an order of clams and fries from the restaurant. "Thanks Winnie." Watkins stood up and closed his door and slowly sat down in his chair. "I want to brief you about a small meeting I had this afternoon with my special projects team. There are three ex-officers that do small projects for us when needed. These guys are retired but still like to help out when they can and these particular ones have seen everything, if you can imagine. One guy takes on, shall we say, a bounty hunter like role and this time he wants the person who killed the Sheriff. He has a background as a sniper and sharp shooter, he is exceptionally good and has always found his mark. Anyhow, this case is just getting way too big so I decided to bring these guys in, turn them loose with the information we have, and see what they come up with. I can not give names, but they will be referred to from time to time. The only reason I even know about these guys is because Sheriff Thompson held three closed door meetings and he wanted me to know about these guys in case something ever happened to him. Who knew? A year ago there a huge cocaine dealer that had arrived here to conduct his business and we passed this on to the guys as a special project. Within a week, the dealer was headed to Los Angeles in cuffs and was sentenced to the chair. It seemed that this guy had killed two Los Angeles police officers.

Enough said. Anyhow, the guys are trustworthy and are a huge help. I briefed them on what you know, but I will need to see them again to update them on what we found this afternoon." Watkins looked down at his desk and stared at a picture of the Sheriff.

Dr. Collins scratched his nose and said, "Would I happen to know them? I have been on this island for almost twenty-five years now. If they are retired I should know them, right?" Watkins didn't say anything. "I guess their identities should be kept secret for their sake?"

"Yes." Watkins looked out his window. "Clyde, level with me. Do you think we have enough evidence to use against this perp to put him away?"

"Well Sam, we are still missing some vital pieces, such as the car that rammed the Sheriff's car. That is a big piece. If we could just find that, the case should be pretty solid, especially if it would have the prints on it to match the person. If not, we can still match the glass chard that we pulled out of the bumper with the car's headlights that should be broken in pieces. That small sliver of glass is what will tie the car and the person to show it was intentional. Any ideas for tracking the car?"

"Well, so far my mechanic buddy hasn't come across a rental car that needs to be serviced. However, if the guy is smart he would probably try to get rid of the car for evidence reasons, so I figure he has hidden it somewhere. I realize the island is small, but there are still a lot of places the car could be hiding. Tomorrow, I will be sending my officers out to look for the vehicle. Hopefully the thing is still in one piece somewhere." Someone knocked on the office door. "Come in."

Winnie walked in with a bag from the *Happy Clams* restaurant. "Thanks Winnie! Here's a tip for you!" Winnie smiled and closed the door behind her. Watkins started to munch on his fries when his pager went off. "Never a dull moment around here." He looked at the number and noticed it was the code for one of the "secret project" guys.

"Clyde, I am going to need you to leave my office temporarily. This phone call is private. It will just be a few minutes." Clyde got up from his chair and went outside his office to talk with Winnie. Watkins dialed the number he had just memorized that morning, "Yeah, what's up?"

"Information for you regarding that car that you are looking for."

"Go ahead."

"The day of the accident, a fisherman was out on the riverside collecting bait and fishing. It just so happened that he saw some guy push his car into a swamp. The fisherman didn't think it was a crime so he didn't say anything. He says people do it with golf clubs all the time. Why not a car? Tonight when we asked him, he spoke right up. You might want to double check it. Later boss." Watkins put the phone down and grabbed his map. He looked for the riverside of the map and then marked down the region where the swampy area was. The region was only about three miles from where Richardson was stationed. Watkins quickly paged him.

Richardson had parked his car in the thick brushy area just enough to camouflage it from the naked eye. He reclined his seat a bit and then pulled out his binoculars. The view from his front seat was perfectly lined up with the back of the MAC truck. He rolled his window down a bit to pick up any possible noise around him.

Just then his pager went off and he picked up his cell phone to call in. "Yes, Watkins?"

"I have some new information for you. About three miles from you is a swampy area. A fisherman saw a guy push their car into the swamp the day of the accident. Don't leave your post, but early tomorrow morning I want you to check it out and verify it. It's too dark right now to see anything, anyway."

"Okay."

"Anything happening out there?"

"Not yet. Just getting myself settled in."

"Page me the second you find something." Watkins ended the call. He sat down at his desk and motioned for Clyde to return. "This day just gets better and better." Watkins explained the new information.

"I will tell the team to be up early as the sun tomorrow. Get some rest, you'll need it." Watkins laughed and smiled. Clyde walked out of his office and headed back to his lab.

*   *   *   *

The men had just about made it down to the very bottom of the steep stairs. Their knees and legs were really feeling it, so each man took a step and tried to stretch their legs out. Jackson was very glad that he had made it to the bottom. A small landing stone was placed before the entrance of the door. Jackson sprawled out on it and reached for his small cotton pillow. "G'night men." Jackson yelled, and turned off his lantern.

*   *   *   *

Milo was tired of watching t.v. There were only four channels that actually worked, so his interest level was quickly decreasing. He walked over to the bedroom, changed into an undershirt, and pulled on some pajama shorts. Then he climbed into bed and set his alarm clock for 6 a.m. He needed to make up for the time that he had wasted today and get the pictures taken so he could leave this wacky island. 'What a bad day,' he thought before he fell into a very deep sleep.

*   *   *   *

Detective Richardson was almost asleep when he heard some tree branches breaking in the far distance. He wasn't sure what was causing the noise but rolled down his window and tried his best to figure it out. The time on his watch showed 4:30 a.m. and he couldn't believe how late it was, but figured anything was possible. The noise seemed to be moving closer and Richardson was getting just a little bit uncomfortable because he didn't know what to expect. He quickly rolled up his window and called Watkins. To his surprise, his line was busy so he put down the phone and figured he would just wait to see what was going on. A bit later, the sounds in the brush had stopped and Richardson figured that the person was walking through the grassy field. This was harder to pin point because there was a light wind out and it was howling softly through the trees. Richardson pulled out his night vision goggles and his camera. He saw the person about one-hundred yards away from him heading toward the truck. He quickly took some pictures through the night scope and tried to zoom in as close as possible, but he had great difficulty with all the brush he was hiding behind. He had to get out of the car in order to get clearer shots, so he tried as quietly as he could to do so. He made sure that the interior light was turned completely off before he opened the door. Thanks to the noise of the wind, he figured he could get away with a small noise from the car door opening so he could tip-toe over to the edge of the brush. To his surprise, the person walking toward him had night goggles on. 'Oh crap!' he thought. If he stayed there he would be seen instantly, so he quietly returned to the car. He knew he couldn't close the door without it making a sound, so he ducked down behind it. The person standing in the field didn't move. Richardson thought he had been seen and grabbed for his gun. Just then, the person began walking straight for him. Richardson backed away toward the trunk of his car. He heard a gun safety sliding off and then the brush started to move ahead of the car. Just then his pager vibrated and he jumped.

CHAPTER 6

▼

Watkins paced around his office waiting to hear back from Richardson. Five minutes went past and he still hadn't heard anything. This worried Watkins, so he decided to take a drive down to the south point of the island. He grabbed his cell phone and paged Richardson again, hoping he would call him back on his cell phone. Just on his way out, his office phone rang. "Your detective was playing hide and seek with me. I had no choice."

Watkins screamed into the phone only to hear the click of the call ending. He ran over to the mounted gun case and grabbed a huge shot gun and four boxes of shells.

"This jerk is mine!" Watkins shouted and ran out to his car. He called three officers on his cell phone and told them to meet him out at the south point beach in a hurry. They all followed his orders. Watkins rubbed the sweat off of his forehead. He had not slept all night, had lost his friend the Sheriff, and now his only detective may have been killed. He was madder than a hornet and determined to catch the guy. It was now personal and if it came to dropping a cop killer, well, it wouldn't be the first body he sent to the morgue.

✳   ✳   ✳   ✳

Troy called Gibson as he approached the center of the island. "We have a small problem."

"What sort of problem?"

"I had to off a cop."

"You did what?"

"He was waiting for me by the truck. I had no choice."

"Yes, you did. You could have gotten yourself out of there."

"No good. We're in too deep and he saw me before I saw him. I thought he had me until he jumped and dropped his gun. Obviously they know about the truck."

"Where is the cop?"

"In the back of the truck under a tarp."

"Get him out of there. His body will trace back to us. Dump the body on the east point of the island and stick to the plan."

"Okay. I'll see you tomorrow like planned." Troy hung the phone up and wiped the sweat dripping off his hair in the chilly pre-dawn air.

✳   ✳   ✳   ✳

By now, the edge of the sun was just starting to slowly creep up to the horizon. Watkins arrived at the south point beach with the three officers following behind him. They quickly jumped out of their cars and ran back into the brush. They came to the field and saw new tire tracks outlining the grass. Watkins cursed and ran over to find Richardson's car. No body was found, but blood was splattered on the trunk and the rear tire. Watkins shook his head, "This isn't happening."

Officer Garret approached Watkins, "Sir, we should probably get a hold of the forensic team and have them check this out."

"They will be here soon anyhow. We got a lead last night about the car that rammed into the Sheriff. We need to drive over there as soon as the team arrives."

"Okay sir."

"Garret, do me a favor. Get a sniffing dog out here and see what we can find. And how about an APB on the MAC truck?"

"Got it." Officer Garret walked off and radioed in for the dog. "Sir, one hour for the dog." Watkins nodded.

$$*\qquad*\qquad*\qquad*$$

In the cabin, Milo's alarm began beeping loudly and caused him to wake up quickly. He turned off the alarm and slowly climbed out of his bed. The day ahead of him would be long because he was determined to take as many photos as possible, do his write up, and then hopefully leave the island in the next two days. He took a shower, shaved, and pulled on some clothes. Next, he loaded up his camera equipment and headed out to his car. On the way out of town, he stopped at the small market and bought a box of cereal bars, a pint of milk, a hoagie for his lunch, a bag of chips, and a six pack of soda. He was all prepared now, and was ready to head down to the south point of the island. In the rearview mirror behind him, he saw a police car coming up fast and noticed a dog sticking his head out of the passenger window. The cop was extremely impatient and actually passed Milo on a double yellow line on a curve. That really upset Milo because he had just been chewed out about driving etiquette. 'I guess if you're an officer you can bend all the rules. Great example,' he thought. Milo grabbed a cereal bar and chewed it vigorously.

*   *   *   *

Jackson's wrist watch was set to beep at 6:30 a.m. When it went off, the sound echoed loudly and everyone was up in no time. They all lit their lanterns and were just about blinded. "Shut up!" Jackson yelled at his watch. "Okay, time to get our day started here. Let's get into this blasted chamber and do our business." He pulled out the wrinkled map and laid it down in front of him. Jackson had to wait until his eyes adjusted before he could read the map. Finally his vision cooperated and he read the first riddle to the door, "The regal is to royal as the lark is to?" he scratched his head. He looked up at the men and said, "The General did not tell me the answer to the riddle before he left, so we're going to have to solve it ourselves."

One of the men spoke up. "Permission to speak, sir?"

"Granted."

"Lark is to spree. A common synonym for the word. I helped the General with it yesterday morning."

Jackson frowned. "Come and answer it for us and show us how this door opens."

"Yes sir." He walked up to the front of the door and placed the side of his face on the door and shouted, "Spree!" The door slowly opened, but just as he was going to enter in, Jackson held him back and then shoved in front of him. The men followed single file behind him, took out their torches, and lit them when the lantern light failed to penetrate the darkness in the large room. The sight of the ancient burial ground was magnificent, and the architecture was amazing. The men were savoring it, but Jackson wanted to move on quickly and get down to business.

"Break yourselves up into three's and stand by the sun, moon, and pyramid symbols. On my count of three you will push your symbol into the wall and then wait for my command." The men ran over to their assigned symbol and waited for Jackson to count. "One, two, three." The symbols all went in exactly like they were supposed to and the gated door to the chamber slowly opened forward. Jackson smiled and walked in. The huge tomb of the Great SHAMBU stood over them like a giant sky scraper.

Jackson pulled out the map from his pocket and read the script in the corner of the map. He walked over to the tomb and found the inscription around the bottom of the tomb was extremely hard to make out. Jackson quickly realized that this inscription contained the seven vital questions. Near his feet sat a pile of heavy, oval shaped stones. In order to place the stones in the great warrior's hand, he would need a ladder just to reach it. At this time, the warrior's hands were raised above his head. He noticed that along the side of the tomb there were numbers marked, two through seven. Jackson assumed that the hands would eventually lower themselves down to the last number. Jackson paced around and cursed. He knew the map had looked too easy. He lit a cigarette and walked around the chamber trying to figure out what to do. The men watched him as he did this.

*   *   *   *

The forensics team and Dr. Collins piled out of the van and walked over to Watkins. Dr. Collins was a bit worried when he saw Watkins looking so frazzled. "Hi, Clyde," said Watkins. "Richardson is dead and we're waiting for the sniffing dog to see if we can find the body."

"So sorry. What can we do?" asked Clyde.

"His car has blood on it. Please have your team get scrapings just to be sure it is his. Also, see if you can follow how far the truck's tires go before they hit the main road. Let's get this done first before we check out the car in the swamp."

"We're on it," Clyde replied. A few minutes later, the officer and the dog arrived. Watkins walked over to the car, opened the back door, and let the bloodhound, Smuckers, out. Smuckers looked eager to begin his job, even though his face appeared naturally droopy. Within minutes, the dog had his nose buried inside the car. After that two of the field agents walked Smuckers down to the field to sniff a few areas. A while later, they had come up with nothing.

Watkins headed over to the beach and unleashed Smuckers. He sat on the hood of his car and looked out at the water. Dr. Collins walked over to him and said, "Sam, you need some sleep. Let me at least get you some coffee." Watkins just stared into space and didn't answer him. In the far distance behind a sand dune, Smuckers started to bark. Watkins ran over toward the dog and stopped dead in his tracks for a moment. Underneath the sand, there were two piles that looked freshly packed. Just then, Watkins saw something out of the corner of his eye. A hand appeared to be sticking above the sand with one ring finger missing.

Watkins shouted, "Garret, summon the team now!" Dr. Collins caught up to him and saw the bodies.

"Unbelievable," remarked Dr. Collins.

"Well, one mystery solved. Now how does it relate?" Watkins remarked.

"We'll try to have that answered sometime today. I'll have the team bag them and tag the one with the missing ring finger. I do believe we have found Mr. Simpson. Back at the lab, we'll take out the bullets and see if we can get any prints from the bodies. We'll be in touch." Watkins nodded and watched Dr. Collins give his team the new orders. A short while later, the team piled back into the van and headed back to the lab.

*   *   *   *

Milo was just approaching the south point of the island, when the forensic team van drove past him speeding at least ten miles over the speed limit. When he arrived at the beach, he saw Officer Watkins and Officer Garret staring at him with very irked faces. Watkins walked over to him and put his hand up. "This beach is closed today. Please turn around and head back to town."

"Hey, I have a job to do too. I need to take pictures for my magazine." Milo yapped back.

"Don't make me tell you to leave again. When I say it is open you can come back. Now get out of here." Milo frowned and backed his car up. His day was starting off badly again. 'What is it about this island?' Milo wondered.

*   *   *   *

It was now mid-morning, and Jackson still had not decided what he should do about the unreadable inscription and the height of the great warrior's hand. Finally, one of the men approached Jackson. "Sir, time has past and we haven't done anything. What is our next move?"

Jackson frowned, paced around, and finally replied, "Men, we have a problem here. The questions we need to answer are going to be very tough to make out. The words appear to be harder to read then expected. This may complicate things a bit, but I have a plan. I decided that seven of you are going to sit here and figure them out, both question and answer. While you remaining three, will need to balance each other so you can reach the hand of the great warrior and place each stone in the hand. Figure out among yourselves which of you has circus talents and start practicing the three-high act! The rest of you, get busy with the questions. While you do that, I will be guarding the stairway because we don't want to be surprised down here and miss our chance. If you are able to answer the questions correctly and you find the gold, I want one of you to get me before you touch it in case there is a trap. Do we understand?" The men nodded as Jackson left the chamber.

＊   ＊   ＊   ＊

Back at the lab, Dr. Collins and his team did an autopsy on the two bodies. They ran a finger print from the John Doe and waited for the match to come up with something. The finger prints had finally matched a man named James Donahue who was an ex-army commander from Vietnam. His closest relative, his ex-wife, lived in Los Angeles. Agent Jacobs called the ex-wife and asked if she wanted to bury him, since she was listed as next of kin on his records. She agreed and made arrangements with Agent Jacobs. Unfortunately, Simpson did not have any relatives listed on his record so they made a few phone calls to the Los Angeles police department and asked what should be done. Under the advisement of Capt. John Carter, the bodies were to be flown to Los Angeles and the morgue would handle it from there. By early afternoon, Dr. Collins had written up the report and made arrangements for the bodies to be flown to Los Angeles. Dr. Collins closed his office door and decided he needed some sleep. He told his team to take a breather and wait until he contacted them. On his way to his car, he called Watkins and gave him an update on his day. Watkins thanked him and told him to keep his cell phone nearby. Dr. Collins put his cell phone away and opened his car door. He climbed into his car and headed to his small beach house to relax for the remaining part of the day.

*   *   *   *

Milo pulled his car over and found a map. He circled the areas on his map that he still wanted to explore on the island. The eastern and the northern points of the island looked quite interesting to him. The east point of the island was closer to him so he decided to go there first. He pulled back onto the main road and drove until the sign pointed to the west point of the island. He turned the other way and a little while later, his cell phone rang.

"Yes?"

"Milo. You didn't answer my phone call from yesterday? What's your problem?" Swanson shouted at him.

"I had a bad day yesterday and I was unable to take your call. But I'm working right now. What's so important?"

"Don't get smart with me. I don't need your excuses and you're temporarily suspended from this project. You don't call in to give updates and I haven't been faxed anything to even prove that you're really working on that island. You're probably in an airport bar in Los Angeles instead. Actually, consider yourself done with this project. The island can rot for all I care."

"But sir, by the end of today I will have pictures for you and I will fax them to you. Just give me to the end of the day. Please. You don't know what it is like here."

"No more excuses, I've made up my mind."

"Listen to me, I will have it for you. You have nothing to lose here. I can't fly back until the end of the week anyhow. What am I supposed to do with all this film?"

"Fine. This is your last chance to save your job. I expect pictures no later than 5 p.m. New York time." Milo quickly calculated when he needed to have them in. A five hour difference in time would only give him three hours to get them done.

"Fine. You'll have them."

Swanson hung up in the middle of the sentence. Milo cursed and started speeding like a maniac over to the east point of the island.

✳   ✳   ✳   ✳

Watkins advised Officer Garret to take the dog back to the station. The other two officers stayed with Watkins, and they all sat down at a nearby picnic table. They opened a map in front of them and Watkins circled two areas. "Okay, the north point and the east point of the island seem to be our only choices for where the truck might be headed. Obviously they aren't going to drive through town on the west point. So, I want one of you to go to the north and the other to go to the east point of the island and check it out. Call me or page me immediately if you see any odd activity or the truck. Richardson could still be alive, so I want you to do your best to find him. These guys are dangerous, so don't get clever, but if you see anyone near the truck, handcuff them immediately. Any questions?" The officers shook their heads and headed over to their cars.

Watkins folded up the map and climbed into his car, started his engine, watched as the other officers took off, and then followed behind them.

*   *   *   *

Milo looked at his watch and started to worry. The east point of the island was about ten minutes away from him and he had already used up a half hour. Finally, he reached his destination and found a small parking lot to park his car. He quickly grabbed his camera bag and made sure he grabbed his digital camera, since there would be no time for him to develop his pictures. Every thirty seconds he stopped to take a picture of a tree, a bird, a winding path, the ocean in the distance, or the clouds in the sky. He was running out of things to shoot, but tried his hardest to take as many pictures as possible. A short while later, he had just about filled his third and last memory card and felt that he had enough pictures for this side of the island. He ran back to his car, pulled his laptop out of his bag, dumped the pictures, hooked up his small portable printer, and printed out four pages of pictures. After he finished all of that he packed everything back up, started his car, and sped off back towards town. Milo checked his watch. He had exactly one hour and thirty minutes left to get back to town and send his pictures to Swanson. Since there wasn't much traffic on the road, he sped ten miles over the limit. As he was coming around a curve, a police officer pulled past him. Luckily, the officer wasn't using radar so he managed to get by without a ticket. Milo gulped. Too close a call though, because getting stopped would use up time he didn't have, so from that point on he went the exact speed limit.

*   *   *   *

Officer Rhinehart sped toward the east point of the island. He arrived where Milo had just been and got out to investigate. The area was peaceful. An occasional bird made some noise, but other than that nothing seemed out of the ordinary. He walked down toward the beach and saw some giant tire marks. They headed off toward the brush and then vanished. The officer called Watkins to report. Watkins told him to get pictures and hike around the area to see if there were anymore leads. Rhinehart grabbed his camera from his car and shot a few pictures of the tracks, then walked into the brush. He noticed something big had come through the area because there were broken trees and bushes around him. As he continued into the brush, he found disrupted soil and one footprint. He took a picture and measured the size of the print, then headed back to the car to get out a small shovel. As he rummaged around his trunk, he heard the radio come on so he went over to it and picked the receiver up.

"Rhinehart"

"Officer Watkins needs all officers to report back to the station by 6 p.m. for assigned duties. Over."

"Okay, please contact Officer Watkins for me right now."

"One moment please."

Rhinehart waited a few seconds then Watkins replied, "Yeah."

"Sir, I followed the truck's tires and they headed into the brush. About twenty yards into the brush, I found one footprint and disrupted soil. I'm just about to see what is underneath the area."

Watkins paused. He wondered what the odds were for Richardson to be under there. His stomach turned into knots. "Okay, hang up the radio and take the cell phone with you. Call me as soon as you turn up anything. I will wait here for your call."

"Will do." Rhinehart put the radio receiver back in its cradle and turned it off. He grabbed the shovel and headed back over to the brush and began to dig the area where the soil seemed disturbed. A couple inches into the ground, he found a blue plastic tarp and as he pulled it back, his suspicions were confirmed. He quickly called Watkins on the cell phone, "Sir, I've found Richardson. He was under a tarp."

Watkins cursed and felt his blood pressure rising. He finally replied, "I will have Dr. Collins and the team come out to meet you. Please wait for them."

"Okay." Watkins was furious. He paced around his office and threw a chair into the wall. Rhinehart said a prayer over Richardson's body, then walked back to his car, and waited for the forensic team.

Watkins finally calmed down enough to call Dr. Collins at the lab, but found that he wasn't there. So he told one of the field agents the latest news and asked for him to update the rest of the team. Watkins then tried to call Dr. Collins at his beach house. The phone rang a few times, but Dr. Collins was so far gone into a deep sleep he didn't hear it. The bottle of whiskey beside his bed probably didn't help his coma-like sleep. Watkins slammed the phone down and tried paging him. Dr. Collin's pager was buried under his clothes on the floor, but it was just loud enough to wake him up for an instant. The pager beeped loudly, half muffled under his clothes, while Dr. Collins rubbed his eyes and tried to remember where the pager was. He got up and walked over to the pile of clothes sitting on the floor and found the pager. Slowly, he grabbed his cell phone and called Watkins.

"Watkins here."

Dr. Collins yawned, "You paged me?"

"Clyde, I have some news for you." Watkins explained what Rhinehart had found.

"Is my team already out there?"

"They should have already left."

"I will meet them out there and look over the body. I should have my report for you by this evening."

"Thanks, Clyde." Dr. Collins hung his phone up, scratched his head, and slowly headed for the shower.

*   *   *   *

Meanwhile, Jackson sat in the stairwell outside the entrance way to the ancient burial ground chamber and lit a cigarette. These plans were not going as smoothly as he had expected. He figured the General had probably overlooked something and obviously the tomb was it. He cursed and frowned. The sleeping gas was still in his duffle bag and he still planned to use it no matter what. He was still wondering how he was going to gas them and close the trap door while they were still in the stairwell. He smiled as his head raced with ideas of killing the men.

Inside the secret chamber, the men were still working on the questions. One of the men pieced his question together and thought he had the right answer. He double checked with the other men and everyone seemed to be in agreement that the answer was "true" to the question referring to grains and plants. One man stood below the great warrior's hand and held up the other man on his shoulders. Then the third man climbed up and balanced himself and put the stone in the great warrior's right hand, marked "truth." They waited and then they heard a creaking noise. The men jumped down from their stances and stood back away from the tomb. The noise got louder and then the entire tomb shook and a large crack began to appear by the foot of the tomb. Above them, they could see the huge warrior's right hand slowly falling downward until it stopped at the second marking. When it stopped, the left hand began to drop until it also stopped at the second marking. The men kept backing away from the tomb until the noise stopped and the crack opened about an inch. Everything became silent again and then the men slowly proceeded forward.

Jackson peered inside the chamber to check things out. "What happened?" One of the men standing near him explained. Jackson studied the crack and then noticed the ceiling also had a smaller crack in it, just as a drop of water hit him on his head. "Men, let's work a little faster. Remember we're on a timed schedule." Jackson walked off disgruntled as usual.

CHAPTER 7

▼

Milo finally arrived back in town with about thirty minutes to spare. He pulled his car in a parking space in the town square and ran out to find a place with a fax machine. He scratched his head. 'Let's see, grocery store, restaurant, hotel, gas station, police station, and chapel. But, where is the copy center?' he thought. He ran over to the police station to find out where he could use a fax machine.

There was a line in front of the clerk, so he tried to walk behind the desk and find an officer. The clerk grabbed his arm and said, "Wait in line. Don't even think about crossing behind this desk."

"But, I need a fax machine."

"There are no public fax machines. Closest to you would be the airport."

"The airport? That's about twenty minutes away from here. I need to use one now."

"Airport or no fax." The clerk pointed to the door and then looked at the next person in line.

Milo screamed. An officer nearby heard the ear piercing yell and he jumped spilling his coffee all over him. The people in the line and the clerk all looked at him as though he was psychotic. The officer grabbed Milo and pulled him into an office. "SIT DOWN!" he shouted. The officer paced around Milo and made him calm down for a few minutes as he cleaned the coffee off his shirt. "What's the problem, son?"

Milo tried to be as calm as he could and replied, "I need a fax machine! My job is on the line."

"What makes you so special?"

Milo started to get fired up and began to yell, "I don't have time to answer your questions. Could you please just let me go? Time is being wasted."

"Listen to me, everyone has their own problems and are trying to do their jobs. Screaming and making a scene is not the way to save yourself. Since I don't want you scaring the townspeople and tourists, I will permit you to use our fax machine, but don't expect anything else from this point on. You understand me?" Milo nodded. "Follow me."

The officer knocked on Watkin's office door, Watkins yelled, "Come in." Milo and the officer walked in and sat down across from Watkins who frowned when he saw Milo. "Geeze, not again."

"Sir, we need to use your fax machine. This man almost had a nervous breakdown in the hallway."

Watkins gave Milo a dirty look. "Well Mr. Snow, you just can't seem to stay out of this police station, can you?"

Milo looked down at his feet and explained his situation. "I'm in a pickle and I need to fax some pictures to my boss in the next few minutes or I'll lose my job. He'll probably run an article about the island with or without my pictures, but it won't exactly come off as a paradise. I'd rather keep my job and write the article myself."

Watkins frowned, "My heart really bleeds for you, with that sob story and all. Get this loon out of my office after he uses the fax machine." Watkins walked out of his office and slammed the door behind him.

The officer frowned at Milo. He ran over to the fax machine and quickly punched the fax number and set his four pages in the machine. When the last page went through he picked up his pages and nervously paced around. He had a few minutes to spare as he waited for the confirmation to display, thanked the officer, apologized for his shirt, and ran out to his car. He wiped the sweat from his forehead and realized how close he was to losing his job, but soon realized he wasn't so sure if that was a good or a bad thing. In his rearview mirror, he saw the *Happy Clam's* sign and decided to get some food. He was in dire need of some good company and had hoped Aerial might be there.

*   *   *   *

Officer Taylor had just come to the north point of the island. As he pulled up to the beach area he noticed a few cars parked by a popular hiking trail and a few families were out picnicking on the beach. In the far distance, he saw a few fishermen out catching fish and some people were in the ocean swimming. Nothing too out of place showed up so far. Taylor changed his flat shoes to his hiking boots and started up the hiking trail. Again, nothing seemed unusual so he just kept a slow pace up through the mountain ridge trail. He pulled out his binoculars and checked out the areas around him. So far, there was no trace of a MAC truck anywhere to be seen. He continued hiking toward the Cynna Ridge. He knew it would be a long walk, so he picked up his pace and headed in that direction. A few hikers passed him and he talked to them briefly. Later on, when he was almost to the highest point of the trail, he paused again to look through his binoculars at the land below. Just as he was focusing on something large hidden behind the brush below the ridge, a biker came flying down the path at him and he lost his balance as he jumped out of the way. His binoculars went flying right over the edge. Taylor cursed and got up. He looked at the brush burns on his palms and tried not to think about the pain that was coming from his ankle. He sat back down and looked at his ankle. It was swelling like a baseball already, and that was not good. Taylor grabbed his cell phone and called for some help. Officer Kirkwood was near the north point of the island and took his call. Kirkwood told him to wait there, assured him he was on his way, and would find him soon. In the meantime, Taylor laid on his back beside the trail and tried to rest. 'What a bad idea to hike alone,' he thought to himself.

*   *   *   *

Dr. Collins finally arrived out at the east point of the island and met up with his team. They had moved Richardson into the van in a body bag. Agent Jacobs showed him the footprint and the tarp used to bury Richardson. "It appears that he was shot in the head, then wrapped in this tarp, and then buried over here." Jacobs stated.

"These people like to bury their guys under the sand and dirt. As though no one would ever find them! However, they are starting to slip up. Is that a gum wrapper lying over there by those rocks?" Dr. Collins asked.

Agent Jacobs walked over to the rocks and took out his tweezers, "Yes. Wonderful. We'll have some prints from this."

"We're fortunate that the guy was careless. I'm guessing he was in a hurry and didn't want to be here very long. That would explain the crummy job he did of filling in the hole." Dr. Collins walked over to the van and gave out new orders to the team. They did as he instructed and then the team headed back to the lab. Dr. Collins got into his car and called Watkins.

"Yeah."

"Hi, we are packing up here and heading back to the lab."

"Great."

"Good news! This time the guy was careless. We found a gum wrapper near the hole. Hopefully we'll find prints. We'll be analyzing them as soon as we get back to the lab."

"Good work. Let me know what you find later today."

Dr. Collins hung up his cell phone and climbed into his car, started his engine, and then followed the van back to the lab.

*   *   *   *

In the chamber, one of the men had figured out the answer to the second question. Like they had done before, the men balanced each other and placed the stone in the left hand of the great warrior, marked "falsity" this time. This time nothing happened. The men stared at the tomb waiting for anything.

"Was it a wrong answer?"

"Not likely. If it's a wrong answer the chamber will fill with water." Just then, the hands slowly moved down to the third marking. After that, another one of the men who had been working on his question figured out his answer. Once again, the men balanced themselves and placed the stone in the right hand. This time the tomb began to shake and the crack began to grow longer. The men backed away from the tomb until it had finished shaking and watched the huge hands move down to the fourth marking. Jackson ran inside the chamber to see what the noise was. He checked out the crack that grew another few inches and then looked above the tomb. More cracks were made in the ceiling and water now dripped faster below the tomb. Jackson walked out of the chamber and back to the stairwell. He lit up a cigarette and grabbed his knife. 'Just four more questions to go,' he thought and smiled.

*   *   *   *

Milo walked into the restaurant and waited to be seated. Aerial walked over and smiled at him. "Just one?" Milo grinned and nodded. He followed her over to the table and sat down. She handed him a menu and waited for him to order something.

"Clams and fries please." Aerial jotted it down on her pad and took his menu. As she walked away from the table, Milo unfolded his napkin and placed it in his lap. He pulled out his cell phone to check his voice mail and was relieved to see that he had none. A while later, Aerial came back and handed him his food and filled his glass with some water. She winked at him and then walked off. Milo dug into his clams and fries and polished them off quickly. He ordered a slice of apple pie and waited for Aerial to come back. "Aerial, I have had quite a day. What time does your shift end?"

"Seven o'clock. You want to do something?"

"You bet! Could you meet me at my cabin, 10A?"

"Sure. See you then." She brought him a slice of pie and his bill. He finished his pie, paid his bill, and left the restaurant. Milo was definitely looking forward to his evening.

*   *   *   *

Officer Kirkwood arrived at the north point of the island promptly. He called Taylor and asked him where he was. Taylor explained his position and Kirkwood began heading up the trail. A while later, Kirkwood's feet were really starting to hurt, since he had forgotten his hiking shoes and his polished flat shoes were pinching his feet. A few minutes later, he couldn't stand the soreness, so he took off his shoes and socks, which was the way he preferred to hike trails when he was off duty anyway. In the distance, he could see Kirkwood sitting on the grass beside the trail waving his arms. Kirkwood shouted, "I'm here!" Taylor saw him and waited for him to get closer.

In the far distance, Gibson watched the officer wave his hands through his binoculars. "Troy you idiot, police are already on the trail. We're just lucky that the officer is injured or he may have continued down the trail and found us. We're sitting ducks here. This is going to attract attention."

Troy cursed back at him. "I parked the truck before dawn. It isn't visible from the trail, okay? They aren't going to find us." Gibson frowned and continued to watch the officers.

"Took you long enough." Taylor yapped.

"I know. Here, I brought you some ibuprofen and a bottle of water. That should ease your pain a bit."

"Thanks!" Taylor wolfed the pills down with the water. Kirkwood pulled Taylor's arm around him and helped him down the trail. It took twice as long going down as it did for them to walk up the trail. Finally, they got back down to their cars. "Can you drive?"

"Don't think so."

"I'll call in for another officer to get your car." He helped Taylor into the passenger side of his car and then called for Officer Garret to bring another officer out to pick up the car. Kirkwood started the ignition, headed away from the hiking area, and finally made it to the hospital.

*   *   *   *

Jackson's cell phone began to vibrate and it made him jump. He banged his arm into the wall and cursed. "What in sam hill do you want?"

"Problems have arisen up here."

"What do you mean?" Gibson explained Troy's carelessness. "I don't believe it. You both are dead when I get back up there. You understand me?"

"Yes sir."

"You leave the truck where it is and make camp on the other side of the ridge. Make sure you close the trap door completely and pull brush over it. Tomorrow when we come back up, you get your butts back over here to uncover the trap door. I'll take care of you tomorrow night." Jackson slammed his cell phone closed and cursed.

In the meantime, two more men had solved their questions. The men balanced themselves and placed another stone in the right hand, but this time, only the right hand moved down to the fifth marking. Next, they placed a stone in the left hand and another rumble began inside the tomb. The crack grew longer, but water was no longer just dripping from above, it was trickling down like a little waterfall into the chamber. Once again, the hands moved down to the sixth marking. The last two questions were vital now, but both of these were the hardest to decipher, and the wrong answer could mean doom if it was placed in the wrong space. This time five men took one question and the other five took the other question. Jackson walked into the chamber and saw the water dribbling in. Just as he stood beside the tomb, three torches beside his feet went out and he grabbed his lighter to relight them. "Are we any closer?"

One of the men spoke up, "Last two questions sir. We are working on them as fast as we can." Jackson frowned and paced around trying not to get his boots wet.

*   *   *   *

Dr. Collins and the team were working quickly to put together their analysis and Agent Jacobs was still waiting for a finger print match from the gum wrapper. Dr. Collins walked over to the print lab. "Any luck?"

Jacobs replied, "Still waiting."

"I will be in my office working on the report. Get me when a match is found." He walked up to his office and sighed.

Another field agent saw Dr. Collins return to his office and called out to him, "Dr. Collins?"

"Yes"

"The bullet from the body came from a machine gun. That's not a common gun on this island, is it?"

"No, not usually. I would have to check with Officer Watkins about that. Did you run a trace on the bullet?"

"Yes. Actually there was more than one bullet. We managed to remove five from his head. It seems he had a steel plate in there and that stopped them from coming out the other side. Not that is did him much good."

"Okay. Make sure you make a note of that and bring up your analysis report to my office."

"All right." Dr. Collins rubbed his temples and then started to type out his report. It was going to be a long evening.

*   *   *   *

As the day was nearing early evening, Milo headed back to his cabin. He decided to take a shower and change into some fresh clothes as he waited for Aerial. In the meantime, he sat down at the small desk in the cabin, pulled out his laptop and started an outline of his write up regarding the island. He had been having such an awful time so far that he wasn't sure if he wanted to put a tourist through his experiences. But he knew he had a column to write with his pictures and the island was quite beautiful, which he couldn't ignore. Even if everyone who visited had all the same hassles he was having, there would still be plenty of people who would want to visit, and even more who would want to read all about it. He poured himself a glass of water and paced around a bit before he was ready to write. Finally, the words came to him and he began hammering away at the keys. A few minutes later, as he was trying to concentrate on a good theme, his phone rang, and his thought vanished. "Dammit!" he yelled. He picked up the phone, while he tried to keep his temper from exploding, "Hello?"

"Hi, it's Aerial. I just got off my shift. This was a bit unexpected but I'm not going to complain. Can I still come over?"

He relaxed a bit and then replied, "Please do."

"See you soon." A short while later, Aerial knocked on his door and Milo let her in. He waved her to the couch, while he grabbed some firewood and started a fire. "How is your work going?"

"Not too bad. I'm working on my write up for the island. It is a nice place, except for those idiotic police officers who are giving me a hard time."

"Yeah, some of them can be jerks at times, especially Watkins. He is the king of jerks!"

Milo laughed, "Glad to know I am not the only one that feels that way!"

Aerial patted his shoulder. "Hey, tomorrow is my day off and I was wondering if you would like to go to the north point of the island with me. There is this great hiking trail that goes down to the Cynna Ridge. I can guarantee you great pictures!"

"Sure, I'd love to go with you. I was planning to go there tomorrow anyhow, so that would be perfect!" They both looked at each other and then cuddled up beside one another and talked a bit about Aerial's day. A short while later they both fell asleep to a Johnny Carson rerun.

*   *   *   *

It was early evening, and Watkins wanted to have a meeting with the officers. He briefed them on the latest information for that day. "Right now our game plan is to continue looking for the MAC truck and the man or men responsible for detective Richardson's death. I want you all out taking shifts tonight on all four points of the island. Tomorrow, we'll be searching the north point of the island since nothing seems to be happening in town, and we have already been to the south and east points. Officer Taylor had some bad luck and ended up in the hospital with a sprained ankle. If anyone finds anything call me or page me immediately. Get moving." After the crew left, Watkins paged the "special project" team and unlatched the side "fire exit" door.

$$*\qquad*\qquad*\qquad*$$

Jackson began pacing around outside of the chamber. The men were taking too long to decipher the questions to suit him. Finally, he walked back into the chamber and tried to make out the words. One of the men working on the sixth question spoke up, "We found the answer, sir." Once again, the men balanced themselves and placed a stone on the left hand. However, to their surprise, the tomb did not shake. Everything was very quiet until the hands slowly moved to the seventh marking. Jackson rubbed the sweat from his forehead. They were now on the final question and the most difficult question to answer. The men pieced together the question as much as they could, but they told Jackson that their answer was a fifty-fifty guess. Jackson pouted and paced around. He read the question they had jotted down, "If one mixes a bird feather, a handful of mud, and a drop of water together, they will have found the cure for poison whey." Jackson had no idea what poison whey was and agreed with the men to take a guess. "I will be outside getting my bags. Go ahead and place the stone in the left hand." Jackson slowly walked out of the chamber, then dashed for the steps, just in case.

*   *   *   *

Watkins heard a knock on his outside "fire exit" door and watched the three men walk in and sit across from him at his desk. He tried not to look surprised at their identities. "When the Sheriff told me about you three, I couldn't believe my ears. Even without knowing who you were, I knew that if I were in his shoes I would NEVER call on you. But somehow things feel very different now. We have some dangerous men roaming the island and we're finding bodies everywhere. We've lost two men so far without even finding out what they are up to, so now I'm thinking it's time to fight fire with fire. Same deal as the Sheriff had, but I'd just like to ask that the next bodies I find don't belong to some tourist that got in the way." Watkins continued to brief the men on the entire day's find-ings and explained what their assignment was for the night. "The north point of the mountain is where I think these men are. As I said, before, I don't know what is going on exactly, but I do know that you three are the best ones to find this out quickly and confi-dentially." The men nodded in agreement. Watkins grabbed a map of the northern point of the island and began marking areas where he wanted the men to stake out. "In addition, I have a hunch that there may be some kind of smuggling going on. The two dead men at the south point beach may be working for someone because they were not locals and they were from the mainland. Also, the boxes we found in the truck were imported fruit boxes. This island has too much fruit, so something is not right. Their military training also bothers me, so we'll assume that these other guys are ex-military as well. So be suspicious of everything. They've already proven that they will kill at the drop of a hat, so be careful. Start out tonight and call me the minute you find anything." The men nodded again, grabbed their maps, and walked out of the office through the side "fire exit" door. Watkins smiled as the door closed behind the men.

*   *   *   *

Agent Jacobs ran into Dr. Collin's office and said, "Match made. A guy named Troy Jones, who is an ex-military police officer, lives in Los Angeles and is the same guy that rented the MAC truck."

"Great work, Jacobs." Dr. Collins quickly paged Watkins.

"Watkins here." Dr. Collins explained what Jacob's found. "Another ex-military guy?"

"Yes." Dr. Collins exclaimed. "Very peculiar."

"Now that we have identified the prints, I want you to take the team out to the south point of the island, call Chuck at the tow station, and bring up the car that is in the swamp by tomorrow morning. Since we were side tracked with Richardson and the two new bodies, we had to put that task on hold for the time being. That car is still evidence and we can't forget about it."

"Okay. I will alert the team to be ready tomorrow morning." "Now, the plan is for me to go out to the north point of the island tomorrow morning and see what I can find."

"Yeah, but make sure you get some sleep first."

"I know!" Watkin's snapped back. "G'night."

Dr. Collin's hung up his phone and yawned. He held a small meeting in the basement of the lab to update his team with the new orders. "Get some sleep. See you around 6 a.m." The team nodded and parted. Dr. Collins grabbed his coat and headed for his car.

CHAPTER 8

▼

Milo awoke out of his sleepy nap and lightly moved Aerial's head off of his shoulder. He laid her down and put a blanket around her, while noticing how cute she looked. While she was napping, he went into his bedroom and thought it was time to start developing some of his film from earlier in the week. He pulled out the first four rolls of black and white film and set them on the bed. Then he laid out his light proof tank with its four stainless steel film spools in his small bathroom, in preparation for the work he had to do in total darkness. Next he took the film into the bathroom, stuffed a towel across the bottom of the door to block out all of the light, and hen he turned off the bathroom light. In complete darkness and working by feel, he transferred one roll at a time onto the spools. He stacked the four spools in the tank, put the cap on, and when he was sure that his film was safely in the tank, he turned the bathroom light back on. He began pouring his chemicals into the tank, carefully timing each step and thinking, 'If I just had a better digital camera, I could have printed all of these pictures with my computer and saved a lot of grief.' A half hour later, he popped the cap off the tank and hung his film out to dry. While the film was drying he screwed in a red bulb in preparation for handling the photo paper, which fortunately isn't anywhere near as light sensitive as the film. He used a hair dryer on his rolls of film to quicken the drying process. Then he set up a portable enlarger to make his prints. He was starting to hurry now, and within an hour he had a healthy stack of prints rinsing under the faucet in the sink. Finally, he tied up four strings across the shower curtain pole and then clothes pinned his pictures along the strings. Just as he was doing this, a knock came from the door. "Uh, hold on."

Aerial rubbed her eyes, "Having a party in there without me?"

Milo laughed. "No, developing film."

"So, I guess this would be a really bad time to need to use the potty."

"Just a minute. Did you forget that I'm a photographer and I need to work sometime?" Milo quickly removed the trays and chemicals and photo junk cluttering the toilet and drained the sink. Aerial smiled and tapped her foot outside the bathroom door. Milo kicked the towel away from the door as Aerial quickly ran in and pushed him out.

As Milo finished putting away his photo supplies, he found two old sleeping bags in a small closet which gave him an idea. Milo yelled, "Meet me on the porch!" He heard the toilet flush, followed by the water running from the faucet.

"Okay!" she shouted. He met Aerial out on the porch and pointed to the sleeping bags. Aerial giggled. They both climbed into their sleeping bags, looked out at the starry sky, and listened to an owl nearby making a hoo-hoo sound. A bit later, they were both sound asleep.

*   *   *   *

Inside the chamber, five more torches went out and the men had to relight them. They were running out of kerosene and knew that they would have to change to their propane lanterns soon. For the last time, the men balanced themselves and placed the last stone in the warrior's left hand. Slowly, the hands moved down to the seventh position and stopped. Everything was quiet. Then the tomb began to shake and finally the crack began to grow again, this time going the entire way up across the front of the great warrior. The ceiling had nearly given way and water was now pouring in very fast. Near the top of the great warrior's head, the crack stopped and then slowly the tomb parted into two pieces.

Inside the tomb, there was a large chest with a padlock and key. On the outside of the chest, there was an inscription that translated into, "**Whoever takes this treasure will be cursed until their death.**" The men all looked curiously at the inscription. Just then, Jackson walked in and saw the treasure chest and yelled, "Back off!" He tried to pull the treasure chest out of the tomb, while ignoring the inscription on the top of the chest, but it wouldn't budge. Jackson grabbed the key beside the chest and tried to open it, but the key wouldn't work, even though it felt like it had clicked something open. At this point, Jackson was so fired up that he grabbed his gun and started shooting the padlock on the treasure chest. The ruckus he made was so loud from the bullets bouncing and slamming into the walls, that no one was able to hear the outer door creaking shut.

The water level in the chamber was beginning to rise up to their ankles. "Ignore the water. Let's get this open." Jackson yelled at the men. They came over to the chest and as a group tried to pull and tug on the padlock clamp. Some of the men tried to use their pocket knives to pick the lock, but nothing would work. Jackson was getting madder than a hornet and yelled, "Grab your shovels." Jackson counted to three and the men slammed their shovels into the sides of the chest. After a few more attempts, their shovels and efforts proved useless. The water was still rising above their ankles now. It seemed that the chest was unbreakable and the padlock was tougher than it looked. The men became anxious.

*   *   *   *

Watkins had not slept for almost forty-eight hours, so he decided to head to his small beach house and sleep for a few hours before dawn. He left his office, got into his car, and drove home. He walked up to the porch and opened his door. His Airedale Terrier, Boxer, was not happy with him and had made a mess of his house. Boxer ran out to the kitchen to see Watkins and barked loudly at him. "Yeah, yeah." Watkins bent over and patted him, found his food dish, and filled it with some canned dog food. Boxer was now content. Watkins felt bad about his dog. He wasn't a good pet owner because of his late shifts and unpredictable schedule, but really enjoyed coming home when he could and having some company. Samuel Watkins was thirty-five, single, an officer for over fifteen years and his last week had been the most stressful he had encountered in a long time. Someone was going to a lot of trouble to really turn his world upside down. It may be a small world to him, but it was all he had. Sheriff Thompson had hired him as soon as he had graduated from the academy in California. He was good friends with him and knew that this island would be a great place for him to be an officer. The big cities scared him with the crime rates and stress. Urchent Island, however, offered him low crime rates, low stress, and a safe place for him to live. Until this past week. Now he felt like he was in a big city with the troubles that had descended upon the island. After he gave Boxer some "tender-loving-care" he changed out of his clothes and fell asleep on his bed with Boxer beside him.

$$* \qquad * \qquad * \qquad *$$

Troy and Gibson paced around their camp. They had done what Jackson said, but knew that he was still really upset with them. His temper was well known, and he usually cooled off almost as quickly as he heated up, but they had seen a darker side lately and were very concerned. Something was brewing. Gibson looked at Troy and said, "We don't need to take this bull crap from Jackson. I'm tired of his threats."

"Yeah, and now we don't even get any gold since he'll probably try to kill us."

"Not me. I say we get him before he gets us."

"How?"

"We could ambush him. What if we take the truck up near the brush, open the trap door, leave the keys in the ignition, and then plant some C4 (explosives) inside the cab? That way, once he starts the engine, 'Goodbye Jackson! Hello gold!' The back of the truck won't blow and while the cab is lit up we will grab a few bags and run like bats out of hell."

"What about the other men?"

"I overheard the General ask about sleeping gas. You do the math."

Troy scratched his head and replied, "Sounds kind of risky though. We can't be sure he has done the deed."

"It will work. Especially since we know what really happened to the General."

"Where will we get the C4?"

Gibson smiled and said, "My shoes, my belt, my suitcase. I never leave home without it." Troy laughed and then looked seriously at Gibson.

"I'm in."

*   *   *   *

The "special project" team (Charlie, Kyle, and Bill) was approaching the northern point of the island in their old jeep. They had taken enough shells and clips to fight a small war. Charlie drove the jeep through a back forest road and dropped Bill off first. Next, Kyle jumped out and gave Charlie a thumbs up. The two men were on foot now and would make great distance over the north point of the island. Charlie drove back through the forest remembering a very old trail that was covered up years ago. He had a feeling his odds were favorably high, but kept it to himself since he liked to be the first one to get the prey.

*   *   *   *

Jackson and his men were starting to tire. They had been trying their hardest to open the chest, but with the water climbing slowly up their pant legs, they needed to rest. Jackson kept pacing around and splashing water all over himself and the others. Finally, out of frustration, he grabbed a torch and slammed it into the chest, impatiently waiting for it to burn a hole. The wooden planks started to smolder and soon you could smell the odor of burnt cedar. Jackson continued to move the torch up and down the planks until they all finally ignited. Luckily, the water level was still below the shelf with the chest, but the smoke from the fire was starting to be a problem since the chamber had no air vents. Jackson found it odd that the smoke wasn't drifting out of the chamber through the entrance way.

"Keep burning this. I will be back." Jackson passed the torch over to one of the men as he quickly walked out toward the entrance way. To his surprise, the door was shut and he was clueless as to how or when it had closed. He felt his blood pressure rising and knew everyone was now trapped. He stared down at his feet and saw his duffle bag and oxygen tank. Suddenly, he realized that he was the only one with his oxygen tank inside the chambers. The men had left their packs in the stairwell. Jackson smiled.

*   *   *   *

Charlie drove in a few miles on the old abandon dirt road he had once used years ago. He followed it until he came to a cliff and pulled the jeep over into some brush. Remembering what had happened to Richardson, he carefully camouflaged it with a few trees and netting. Next he grabbed his bag and put on his night vision goggles. He would go on foot from here. It was a very humid, warm night and rain clouds swarmed over the northern point of the island. A while later it began to rain. Charlie pulled on a poncho and kept hiking deeper and deeper into the brush. As a child, Charlie use to play in these woods and he knew a few shortcuts to different places. He was glad his mind was still sharp for his age. He passed a huge pile of rocks and recalled the time his friend named it

"Fort Niles," back when they played there years ago. Despite the moss and overgrown brush, he still recognized the fort. Ahead of him, he saw the Cynna Ridge and wondered what kind of activity he might find near the ridge. So he proceeded closer, thankful that the rain would cover the little bit of noise his passage made.

Bill and Kyle shared the same trail for a few miles but then decided to split up and take different routes. Bill headed up the trail as Kyle headed down the trail toward the Cynna Ridge. A while later, Kyle adjusted his night vision goggles and found an abandoned MAC truck hidden quite well under some brush. He paged Watkins.

*   *   *   *

It was almost 5 a.m. when Watkin's pager went off and startled Boxer. Watkins felt around for his pager on his bed, while his dog yapped loudly at the sound of it.

"Quiet!" He pushed Boxer off the bed and stretched over to his night stand to grab his cordless phone. Boxer paced around the bed watching Watkins dial Kyle's number.

"Yeah"

"Yeah, yourself. What's up?"

"Your MAC truck is sitting at the bottom of the Cynna Ridge."

"Good work."

"I'm setting up my equipment now and will stake it out."

"Okay, I will be out in that area this morning. Watch for me. Don't blow your cover."

"Got it. Out"

Watkins hung up his phone and put it back on his night stand. Boxer wanted out and fed, so he got up, stretched a bit, grabbed

Boxer's leash and headed outside with him. Slowly, he tried to figure out what was going on near the Cynna Ridge. A little later, Watkins returned home, fed Boxer, took a shower, got dressed, and was on the road heading into town. The sun was now rising at a steady pace. His only hunch was that something was being smuggled off the island and today was going to be payday.

✳   ✳   ✳   ✳

As the sun grew brighter, Milo and Aerial both woke up at the same time, trying to shield their eyes from the bright shining light. "Inside, quick!" They both jumped out of their sleeping bags, ran inside, and fell onto the couch beside each other. Milo yawned.

"I slept like a baby. How about you?"

Milo smiled, "Yes, I admit it was one of my better sleeping nights. Of course, it was probably because I knew you were right beside me!" Aerial blushed. "Hey, I'm starving! How about you?"

"The restaurant opens in about ten minutes, let's get some breakfast." Aerial got up from the couch and walked over to his bathroom and shut the door behind her. Milo changed his shirt and grabbed his camera gear and photos. Aerial finished washing up in the bathroom and came out. She saw Milo holding a manila folder and his camera bag. A little while later they were ready to go over to the restaurant, eat breakfast, and then head to the north point of the island.

"Let's go!" They walked out of the cabin and over to the restaurant. "I have some neat photos to show you."

Aerial smiled, "Can't wait to see them." As they walked in front of the restaurant, Officer Watkins pulled up right beside the restaurant and jumped out of his car. As Milo went to open the door for

Aerial, Watkins ran right into him from the other side, and the file folder with all the pictures fell to the ground.

"Quick get the pictures!" Milo yelled.

Watkins cursed and stooped down to help pick up the pictures. He started to hand them to Milo until he saw something beside his thumb on the photo.

"What is this a picture of?"

Milo tilted his head to see the photo. "Let's see, I took this in the center of the island in the forest near the waterfall two days ago. I was trying to get a closer look at these blurred things through the brush a ways away from me so I zoomed in with my camera and in the process accidentally took a picture of these men training."

"Men training?"

"Yep, looked like military. About ten men were running in place, stretching, and exercising. I assumed it was a military drill."

"Yeah, that would be a good assumption if there was a military base on the island, but there isn't."

"Oh."

"Can I keep this?"

"Go ahead. It's just a waste of good photo paper as far as I'm concerned."

Aerial stared at Watkins and said nothing. "Aerial, nice to see you.

She replied, "Have you two met already?"

Watkins laughed, "Oh yes, what a trip!" In response to the sarcastic remark, Milo put his arm around Aerial and took her into the restaurant. As she turned her head back to look at Watkins, she stuck her tongue out at him and winked.

Watkins sighed, got into his car, and decided he wasn't hungry for a bagel anymore. Instead, he knew he had a few phone calls to make and the sooner the better.

*   *   *   *

Charlie sat down to take a rest. He had been hiking all night and he needed a break, so he got out his map and decided to plan his next move. The rain had finally stopped by morning, so he took off his poncho and folded it up. In the distance he heard birds chirping and an occasional woodpecker hammering his beak into a tree. Charlie grabbed his binoculars and started looking around, but everything seemed peaceful and still. He lit a cigarette and guzzled some water out of his canteen. A while later he had finished his cigarette and was ready to hike around the bottom of the Cynna Ridge. This time he had his semi-automatic loaded and ready just in case. He sensed danger lurking ahead.

*   *   *   *

Troy and Gibson began to pack up their camp from the night before. Gibson got out a chunk of his C4 block and decided to test the range of the explosion. Not, that he needed to, of course. His training had been very thorough and he liked to play with any type of explosives that he could get his hands on. He hooked a cap to some wire, stuck it into the C4, and connected a switch to the battery. This would be used to send the energy down to the wad he made. He stuffed it in a hole under a bush. "Troy, get away from there. I don't feel like scraping up your remains." Gibson counted down from five and pushed the switch. The bush lifted and blew apart with a loud thump. The noise caused a huge flock of birds to fly off in a pack screaming and chirping like crazy. A few seconds later, they headed into the deep forest where Charlie was hiking.

*   *   *   *

Meanwhile, in the chamber below the Cynna Ridge, the water was continuing to fill the chamber and the treasure chest was still inside the tomb. By the time Jackson had returned, the air was hard to breathe and the men were coughing. However, the planks were becoming weak enough from the blazing flames so that Jackson was able to knock a shovel through two of the planks and soon shiny gold coins were pouring out through the hole. The men quickly grabbed their sacks and began filling as many as they could. Jackson was thrilled as he watched the gold coins pour out. Even though the water was still rising over their knees, the men and Jackson were too happy to care. Finally, as the water was reaching waist high, the men were just about finished collecting the gold. Jackson grabbed his huge sack and finished filling it to the brim. As the last coin in the chest finished spilling out, something odd started happening to the tomb. The two hands of the great warrior started to lift back up toward the top. Jackson was not liking this one bit. He noted that the ceiling above the tomb was already streaming with water and if the hands got too close to the ceiling the walls would give in. Jackson watched as the hands went above the head of the tomb and did not stop where they had once been placed. Instead, the hands slammed up into the ceiling and lifted a huge slab and tons of water came crashing down. Jackson headed outside the secret chamber into the burial ground chamber. Sadly, less than half of the men followed because the others were unable to move. The walls had collapsed on seven of them and they were now under the water drowning and unable to free themselves from the heavy rock slabs. The other men tried to help them, but nearly drowned themselves trying to do so. Jackson began to panic a bit. The three that escaped joined him in the outer chamber. "Do not panic men. We will figure something out." One of the men approached Jackson, "Sir. Once the inner chamber fills up, the water will force itself in here. I think we should try to close the gated door." Jackson agreed. Each man stood in front of the symbols and on Jackson's word they all tried their hardest to push the symbols into the wall, but it was no good. The weight of each stone required at least three men. At this point, the water was slowly approaching their chests. Jackson was running out of time.

▼

CHAPTER 9

Watkins put his foot on the gas and headed as fast as he could to the north point of the island. He called Kyle, Charlie, and Bill to update each of them about the situation and urged them to be as attentive and ready as they could be. He was satisfied with all of his reports from them. However, the flock of birds from Charlie's reports reminded him of what Milo said he had heard a few days ago, which really bugged the hell out of him. He cursed under his breath and continued to speed faster down the highway.

*   *   *   *

Milo sat Aerial down beside him and they ordered pancakes and orange juice.

Aerial smiled, "Hey tiger, what happened out there? Did Sam make you feel a little insecure?" Milo looked annoyed. "Don't worry, we aren't a couple anymore. Sam is way more job oriented than relationship committed." Milo wasn't sure he wanted to know about that. Aerial smiled, "No reason to be jealous."

"Yeah, I know, I am pathetic."

She patted his hand and said, "No, cute." Milo blushed and took a sip of his orange juice. From that point on, Aerial and Milo held hands and had a nice breakfast. After the plates had cleared, Milo handed her his photos and asked her to pick her favorite two out of the pile. She handed the two to Milo and made a note of the ones she liked. After they finished eating and paying the bill, they walked back to the cabin and Milo opened the car door for Aerial. They were now ready to start their wonderful journey to the north point of the island. Or so they thought!

$$*\qquad*\qquad*\qquad*$$

Dr. Collins was already at the lab assigning tasks to his team. They all piled into the van and the driver headed for the highway. Dr. Collins followed behind the van in his own car, and following him was the flat bed tow truck. A while later, they arrived at the spot where the car had been found under the filthy swampy water. The rain from the evening before made things very soggy and the van's rear wheels appeared to have been stuck in the mud. One of the men took pictures of the area where the car was while two of the field agents dove down under the swampy water and attached the tow cables to the frame. Both agents came back up from the water with mud and algae all over their bodies. Dr. Collins had brought two huge jugs of fresh water with him, so that the agents could use them to rinse off the mud. Shortly after that, the car, which was a new BMW, came up from the bottom covered in mud and algae. The team waited for the water to drain from the car and then used a crowbar to smash a window so they could open the door. Water rushed out and their hopes of finding any fingerprints faded. However, the glass from the headlights was what they really needed to match to the crime scene anyhow. The car was a rental. The *Urchent Island Car Rental* metal plate was still fused to the bumper and this would be key information to trace who had rented the BMW. Dr. Collins quickly grabbed his cell phone to find the driver who rented it. His battery was quite low on his cell phone, so he shut it off instead of calling. He knew too well what happened when the low battery light would comes on. It would never fail, just as he would get to an important part of the conversation, the battery would give out and the range would drop to zero. Agent Jacobs noticed his actions and handed him his own phone.

"Just in case, sir."

"Thanks, Jacobs." Dr. Collins punched in the number for the local car rental place. "Urchent Island Car Rental, how may I help you?"

"I need the name of someone who rented a four door, standard, black BMW, current year model. This information is needed for a crime scene as ordered by Officer Watkins."

The customer service lady replied, "Just a minute." He heard some typing in the background. Finally she said, "Before we can give you this information, I will need Officer Watkins to authorize this in person. Please understand this customer used a pro-tected-name policy to keep his identity from anyone but the local police. This is used for certain clients and only when we have autho-rization by Officer Watkins can we give out the information."

"Okay. I understand your position. But, just so you know, we just pulled your BMW out of a swamp and it is no longer in service, if you know what I mean."

The lady gasped. "Is the driver okay?"

"In addition, this particular car is what was used to run Sheriff Thompson off the road. Your BMW will be in our lab from this point on, and when we do release it, your boss will have to come for it in person because of our own protected-name policy. Unless, of course, you would re-consider giving me the name of the driver over the phone so we can continue trying to find the killer."

"Oh my goodness! Sheriff Thompson was like a saint to me, and I'll do whatever it takes to help. Just a minute." Dr. Collins smiled. He knew how to bend the rules. He was good at it, and he enjoyed doing it. "The car was signed out to General Frank Johnson."

"Military eh? Is that why it is a protected-name policy?"

"Sometimes high ranked military officials like to keep their names protected when visiting our island. We mainly use this policy for military officers and diplomatic visitors. It is vital that the local Sheriff sees us in person to request information for security reasons."

"Okay thanks. I will be sending a letter to your office regarding the rental car evidence so that you can process a lawsuit if your company feels compelled."

"Okay."

Dr. Collins ended the call, then said, "Jacobs, how about one more call?" Jacobs smiled and nodded. Dr. Collins called Watkins.

"Yeah"

"We just brought up the car from the swamp. Turns out it was a rental. I called the car rental place and found out that a military General somebody-or-other had rented it. Did you know that military officers like to keep their names protected and usually only authorized Sheriff's or Officers are permitted to know?"

"Actually, I just heard about that new policy coming into effect this year. It has something to do with keeping troop movements secret or something like that. Well, in addition to this General who must be the ring leader, we also have ten men under him." Watkins explained the entire incident that happened with Milo and his special project team. "Okay. Well, I'm almost at the north point of the island now, so I need to go. I will contact you later today. Load the car and take it back to your lab and do your report. Also, when I get back, make sure your remind me to give you this picture of the men training. I'm sure it will be key evidence for something."

"Okay." Dr. Collins hung up and handed the cell phone back to Jacobs. Next, he gave out his orders for the team to analyze the car and reminded them to meet him back at the lab later that day. Dr. Collins thought it was odd for the military to be involved in something sinister like running the Sheriff off the road to his death, but yet things were still not adding up. This lab case was getting more complex each day and he was ready for a good stiff drink.

*   *   *   *

Jackson and his men took out their pocket flashlights to use as the blackness began to creep over them. The torches had gone out, and the uplifting sense of adventure went out with them. All that was left was the cold, wet, dark, and dread. By now, the water was slowly rising above their chests, so Jackson ordered the men to try opening the door. One of them felt a shovel lying on the floor below his feet. He bent down to reach for it and completely immersed himself in the water. He came back up quickly from the ice cold water and handed it to the other men. For a short while, the men leaned into the shovel and tried their hardest to pry the door open. Jackson moved off in the corner of the chamber. He had dragged his duffle bag and oxygen tank with his feet over to him and wrapped the oxygen hose around his right arm, keeping it below the surface of the rising water. The water was just about up to their chins now and the three men started to panic. Jackson watched as they began to scream and claw at the door. It was no use. A short while later everything was quiet except for the sound of Jackson sucking the oxygen from the tank. The water slowly rose above Jackson's head as he treaded water and waited in the pitch black, cold, water hoping he would have enough oxygen to give him a time to find a way out.

*   *   *   *

Troy and Gibson had begun hiking back around the Cynna Ridge toward the MAC truck. Gibson was ready to wire up the truck with his C4. In the far distance, Gibson thought he saw someone so he grabbed his binoculars and focused them to see what was ahead of him. Sure enough, he saw Charlie hiking in their direction. "Get your gun ready, and follow my lead." Troy did as he was told. They split up around the brush and hid behind two trees across from each other. As Charlie was approaching, Gibson quietly pulled his machine gun strap around his head. As he walked past the tree, Gibson's fist met Charlie's face. Charlie fell down stunned. Gibson quickly waved to Troy and he stood above him with his gun pointing at his head. Charlie tried to reach for his semi-automatic, but it was too late. Gibson had found it first.

"Hmm. You don't look like a tourist, do you." Gibson slapped his cheek as Charlie started to squirm. Troy put his foot over his neck and pressed the barrel of the gun on his forehead. "Don't even think about it." Charlie had no choice at this point but to go along with the two thugs. Troy gagged and blindfolded him, then tied his hands up to a rope which they pulled as they walked. Charlie overheard one of them dialing a cell phone and saying, "Yeah. Got one of yours. This complicates things. Out." The thug seemed really upset and he wondered who the guy had called.

*   *   *   *

Watkins had been making great time on the highway, until he came to a fork in the road where there had been a small fender bender with two cars. He rolled down his window and asked the two people if anyone was hurt. Luckily, no one had been hurt and it was a minor accident, so he called Officer Garret to help out. He sped away and finally made it to the north point of the island. He pulled over near the hiking trail and called Kyle to find out if anyone had returned to the MAC truck yet. Kyle replied that it had been fairly quiet in the morning and that he was still watching and waiting. Watkins asked for his position so he could meet him. As Kyle spoke, Watkins marked down the area on his map and then ended the call. Next, he called Bill and told him where he would be and asked him to meet him near that area. Bill agreed with the new plan and told him he would be there. Finally, he called Charlie, but to his surprise, he got voice mail immediately which meant the phone was turned off. Watkins rubbed his forehead and called Kyle back. This time, his phone was off too. Watkins didn't like this at all. He got out of his car and went behind it to open the trunk. Inside he grabbed his hunting rifle and a small bag of shells, making sure his rifle had a full magazine.

*　　*　　*　　*

Milo and Aerial were also making great time on the highway, since it was still early enough in the day for them to not encounter too much traffic. On the way, they saw a fruit stand where Aerial wanted to stop by and pick up some fruit and trail mix. Milo pulled the car over and let her out. A short while later, she came back with two arm-fulls of pineapples, papayas, and a bag tied over her arm with dried fruit mix. Milo quickly jumped out of his seat and ran around the side of the car to open the door for her.

"Thanks!" Aerial smiled at him as she carefully set the fruit and bag in the back seat. Milo closed the door behind her and then got back into his seat and pulled the car away from the fruit stand. "Want to try a papaya?"

Milo raised his eyebrow. "Never had it. Sure." Aerial grabbed a small papaya from behind her and handed it to him.

"Just sink your teeth into it like a pear." Milo did so and thought it was very sweet, almost like cantaloupe.

"Good!"

"The Hawaiian variety of this has a better flavor then the Mexican variety. Try tasting the seeds."

Milo sucked a few seeds and then started to cough. "Spicy!" He grabbed a three day old can of warm lime soda and tried to wash down the seeds. "Ack! This soda is nasty." Aerial laughed while watching his reaction. Milo frowned and finished his papaya.

*   *   *   *

In the chamber below, Jackson was still hanging in the water and trying hard not to think about how much air he had left. All of the sudden, he heard a rumbling sound in the water. He felt the flow of water shift below his head. A minute later his feet touched down. As soon as the water level fell below his chin, he yanked off his oxygen tank and took a breath of fresh air. A short time later all of the water had drained from the chamber and he stood in the middle of the outer chamber shivering from his wet clothes and wondering about the people who had rigged this place. He walked into the inner chamber and saw the men all lying belly up or on their backs completely dead from the water in their lungs. Above him he noticed the tomb and saw that the two large hands had dropped back into their original place. The slab of rock was now put back into place and the water was just about finished draining. The sacks of gold were still on the floor in the chamber so he began moving them carefully into a pile. The water added a little more weight to them, but at this point he didn't care how heavy they were since he was alive and rich. To him, nothing else mattered. However, he was still annoyed about the locked door so after he finished piling up the sacks near the door, he sat down and took a rest. The exercise and fresh, dry air had helped him warm up. He looked around and spotted something shiny at the base of the tomb, so he stood up and walked over to it. To his dismay, it was the treasure chest key. He rubbed his head and started to walk away from it, but then frowned as he remembered something. When he had turned the key in the padlock he had heard a clicking sound and wondered if that could have triggered the door. He turned back around, picked up the shiny key, and jammed it into the padlock. This time he turned it to the left instead of the right. Everything was quiet and he cursed. Then he tried it again, turning it to the right this time, and seconds later he heard a creaking noise. He ran out to the entrance way to see the door. Sure enough, the door had opened. Jackson was thrilled. He pried the door open the rest of the way and walked into the stairwell. Next he looked at his watch to see how much time he had before Troy and Gibson would meet him. He smiled and then started to tie four sacks of gold together with some rope. Finally, he was ready to start back up the stairs carefully moving his gold two steps at a time with him to the top. The heavy lifting didn't bother him at this point because all he could see were dollar signs. Slowly, he began his journey.

*   *   *   *

Gibson and Troy had arrived back to the place where their truck was sitting. They opened the back of the truck and pulled Charlie inside. They covered him in a tarp leaving just barely enough breathing room. Charlie had to act fast. He tried his hardest to move but it was no good. Every moveable part of his body was tied up, so instead he decided to wait and conserve his energy. He slid his ear beside the plastic and tried his best to hear what was going on. Gibson yelled at Troy, "Get the hood open. I need to start wiring this up." Troy walked over to the front of the truck and started to pop the hood open. Gibson was putting his wires and switches together and cutting his C4 block into three large chunks. Above the huge truck, Kyle watched from his post.

*   *   *   *

Watkins had been hiking on a trail for a while. He took a small break, sipped some water from his bottle, and wiped the sweat from his face. After his short rest, he grabbed his binoculars and looked down below the ridge. The trees and brush were so overgrown that he couldn't make anything out. Above him, he could see Bill making his way down the sharp rocks. He continued walking onward and finally met up with Bill. Watkins waved to him while Bill took a rest on the trail. "Those rocks are quite a work out for me." Bill said half huffing.

"I can imagine."

"What's our next move?"

"I would like to go down and see what is going on at Kyle's post. Is your gun loaded?"

"Yes"

"Good. Let's get moving." Watkins and Bill headed down the trail a bit farther before they started down the sharp rocky cliff.

*   *   *   *

At the north point beach, Milo parked his car and got out a map of the area. Aerial jumped out of the car and yelled, "Okay, This is a really fun area!" She pointed to a few places on the map Milo was holding. "My friends and I used to come out here and hike all the time. You up for a little hiking and rock climbing?"

"You bet!" Milo grabbed his bright blue backpack and filled it up with two cameras, a water bottle, a towel, and his map.

"What's the towel for?"

"I use it to pad my cameras in case I bump the backpack into something. Remember, cameras are my life!"

Aerial laughed and grabbed a papaya and a handful of dried fruit mix from the car and stuffed it in her baggy coat pockets. They began walking up the trail and Milo began taking pictures of Aerial and some birds. Aerial waved for Milo to follow her, "I know a shortcut, let's go!" Milo put away his camera and followed her down a rocky cliff. A little bit later they found a huge pond filled with yellow and orange fish. Aerial kicked her shoes off and waded into the pond. Milo wasn't too sure about the idea, because the size of big fish and his small toes bothered him. "Come on in chicken!" Aerial yelled while splashing some water on Milo. He stood away from the pond and got out his camera. He figured this would make a great picture and it gave him an excuse to stay out of the pond. Milo took a few pictures of the water, the fish, and Aerial dancing knee deep in the pond. Just as he laid his camera down on a pile of rocks, he tripped over his shoelace and fell face first into the pond. A huge orange blur swam past his nose. He quickly got up from the pond and began to curse. Aerial laughed until Milo finally told her to take a hike. He dug out his towel and started to dry himself off, then felt around his pocket for his comb.

Aerial came out of the pond and tried her best to stop laughing, "Milo you are a nut!" Milo didn't look happy. She held his hand and helped him wring out his shirt. As they got up from where they were sitting, Milo looked at Aerial and said, "Think it's funny, eh?"

She nodded, then grinned wickedly and said, "Now I get why you carry the towel. You're a klutz!" As Aerial turned away from him, he gave her a firm tap on her shoulder and decided it was her turn to see the big fish up close. Aerial gave a slight shriek as she fell into the pond. A huge yellow fish swam over her face before she could sit upright. Milo laughed and took pictures of the event. Aerial replied, "Okay, okay, you got me. I guess I deserved that. Help me up!"

Milo backed away shouting, "No way!" and ran away from the pond. Aerial got up and ran after him, calling him everything from a louse to a turkey, but that just made him laugh as he ran deeper into the brush.

*   *   *   *

Jackson was beginning to tire. He had quite an ordeal in the chambers and he needed to rest, since he had missed out on a full night's sleep. He would have killed for a cigarette, but they were all wet and useless. In his pocket, he felt for his cell phone and figured it was time to find out what was going on above ground. He dialed Gibson's number, noticing his signal was very weak. He did his best to yell over the static, "What's going on up there? And speak up, I hardly have a signal."

Gibson shouted as loud as he could, "Not much. Just waiting here for you."

"Good. I will be arriving late this afternoon."

"Really. So soon?"

"Plans have changed a bit down here. Don't question me."

Gibson paused. "See you soon boss."

"Not so fast." The phone ceased for a second and Jackson had to wait. "Open the trap door now, but keep the brush still over it. I want to see daylight."

Gibson yelled for Troy to do just that. Jackson impatiently waited to see a crack of light. "What's taking so long?" Gibson said nothing. "You droit, what is going on?" Once Troy had finished opening the trap door, Jackson's cell signal grew a little stronger. "Finally. See you two later." Jackson slammed his phone shut. From where he was sitting on the steps, he could just see a few thin rays of daylight almost as a softer darkness in the pitch black, but it was just enough to keep him motivated.

$$* \qquad * \qquad * \qquad *$$

Above ground, Troy and Gibson had finished wiring the truck. Gibson shouted to Troy, "Oh yeah, this will fix him." Troy nodded and stood like a statue by the truck. Kyle had watched them finish wiring the truck and decided to have some fun. He saw a pile of huge rocks and had a plan to distract the men long enough so that he could steal some of their C4. Kyle grabbed a huge rock and then threw it as far as he could over his shoulders. The rock made a lot of ruckus and both men looked in that direction and started to mosey away from the truck. Kyle slunk down the bank and carefully slid under the engine. He disconnected the wire and began to pry loose the C4. He saw the men's feet coming closer toward the truck and quickly grabbed what he could and headed up the bank. Neither man spotted him as he got back to his camouflaged post. He smiled looking at his new toy. Most people would have just stayed in hiding, but he figured, 'What good is sniper training without a bit of fun?'

*   *   *   *

Watkins and Bill continued down the rocky cliff. Bill lost his footing and slid down a few feet, bruising his shoulder. "Bill, you okay?"

Bill looked up at Watkins, "Never been better!" Just then, Watkins lost his footing too and came crashing down into Bill.

"That was a hell of a thing." Both men laughed and then tried to find better footing. "These cheap hiking boots really bite. Last time I order them from 'we-like-to-hike.com'" Watkins stood up and stretched. His back hurt and he had a nasty brush burn on his arm. He grabbed his binoculars and tried to see if he could find where Kyle was stationed. "These directions just don't seem right. According to this map, Kyle should be below this ridge. I don't see him at all."

Bill grabbed his binoculars and looked over at the ridge. "Yep, Kyle is good. Almost didn't see him under that tree limb. A little breeze happened to move that limb and I saw his black netting."

"Good job." They slowly headed off the rocky cliff and began hiking into the brush.

*   *   *   *

Milo and Aerial began walking deeper and deeper into the woods. They had retrieved Milo's cameras and backpack, and by now their clothes were almost dry again. Milo was starting to worry how lost he was getting, but was just glad that Aerial knew her way around.

"Hey, ever play paintball?"

"I am the king of paintball! Guess I forgot to mention that it is something I do as a hobby in between photo shoots. Sometime I will teach you how to do it my way!"

"You're on! Want to do it now?"

"Huh?"

"Follow me!" Milo was surprised. He followed Aerial and tried to ask her what she was talking about but she just ignored him. A short while later they approached a small wooden shack. Aerial told Milo to stay outside, but assured him she would be right back. She climbed in through a window and he heard a lot of noise. Eventually, she came back out the window with two ugly guns and two brightly colored bathrobes in her hands. Aerial smiled at him and said, "Put this over your clothes. If I shoot you I don't want you to get messy." She handed him the gun and slammed a colored pack of balls into it. Milo looked hilarious in the bathrobe but he didn't care. He was out to have fun. They both ran around the forest hiding behind trees trying to get close enough in range to hit one another. Aerial hit Milo a few times before he colored her entire front side orange and red. Milo ran out of paintballs, but continued to act as though he had a full gun. All afternoon they ran around the forest acting like little kids, but to Aerial's surprise, Milo was better than she was at the game. Aerial came up from behind the tree that Milo was standing at and said, "It's just me now. You are empty and I am not. Going to surrender?"

"Never!" Milo grabbed for Aerial's gun so quickly that he had it in his hands facing her.

"How did you do that?"

"I saw it in a movie once and just wanted to see if I could do it." Aerial laughed as Milo painted her robe blue.

CHAPTER 10

▼

Troy walked around to the back of the truck and sat down. Charlie was still listening attentively and trying to piece things together. He had hoped Kyle was still watching the truck and had seen the thugs put him inside. However, he was a little bit curious as to why Kyle hadn't taken these men down yet, since Watkins had ordered them to be arrested on the spot. This didn't make sense to him so, he continued to patiently wait until something happened, even though he still had a gut feeling something was very wrong. Troy grabbed a bag of snacks he had packed and began munching loudly on some chips. He looked at his watch, "How much longer do we have to be out in this humid, buggy environment?"

Gibson smiled as he replied, "A few more hours and then it will all be over. I'm going to charter a personal private plane out of here tomorrow and then off to the Caribbean. I need a nice long vacation." Charlie made note of that just in case he had to track him down after this was over or whatever was going on.

*   *   *   *

Watkins looked at his watch. "Why don't you go over to Kyle's post and relieve him for a bit. I'll meet you there a bit later, okay." Bill nodded and watched Watkins hike down another ridge below.

Bill slowly approached Kyle, trying not to startle him, so he quietly walked over to the netting and climbed underneath it. Just as he did this, he saw Kyle holding a chunk of C4. "Hi Bill!"

"Hey, what's going on?"

"I need you to do something for me. I need you to check out and see if Charlie is in the truck down there. Two thugs came back with a guy looking like Charlie. I can't leave my post, but I need to make sure we don't make a mistake and blow Charlie accidentally. I'll cover you as you go down."

Bill carefully left the post and slid down the bank. Troy and Gibson were sitting on the back of the truck so Bill tried carefully to not make himself seen. He slid under the truck and stayed there until he saw the men start to move away from the back of the truck. He looked up above the engine and saw some interesting wiring with a few C4 blocks stuffed in between the wires. He figured this was Kyle's work, so he left it alone. As he slid his body under the middle of the truck, both men moved and walked away. This was his chance to peer into the truck and look for Charlie. He slid under the bottom of the back part of the truck and then jumped into the back. He saw a tarp and some crates but didn't see Charlie. He walked in a bit closer and just then the truck door came crashing shut. The thugs had seen him and now he was locked in and trapped. There was hardly any light so he sat down and tried to find his lighter. Just then he heard a noise coming from the front of the truck. Bill clicked his lighter on and heard a muffled noise.

"Charlie?" A large thud sounded as Charlie tried to bang his body on the floor to answer Bill. In the dim light, Bill crawled closer toward the front of the truck and felt around. He saw a plastic tarp and then Charlie's head. Quickly, he pulled the cloth from Charlie's mouth that had gagged him and pulled his blindfold off. "Charlie?"

"Yeah."

"What happened?" Charlie explained the entire event to him. "Drat. Well, at least I got my gun so we should be all set, and Kyle knows where we are, so we are in good hands." Bill pulled his gun out and took his safety off. They sat quietly in the dim light and waited patiently for the back of the truck to open.

*   *   *   *

Below the trap door, Jackson was slowly making his way up the steep staircase with his gold sacks and lantern. As he made his way up, the cracks of the sunlight seemed brighter and brighter to him. By now he was over half way up. He stopped to rub the sweat off of his face. His clothes had finally dried out, but now they were starting to get wet from sweat, and he couldn't wait to be out of the dingy stairwell.

*   *   *   *

Watkins had decided to look for Charlie, so he had wandered through the deep woods to try and find him. He checked his map and went to where Charlie was supposed to be, but to his dismay, he wasn't there. Watkins sat down on a rock and wiped the sweat from his forehead. He picked up his cell phone and tried to call Kyle again, and this time the phone was ringing.

"Kyle?"

"Yeah."

"What's going on. Is Bill with you?"

"I sent him to find something for me."

"Oh. How come your phone was off earlier?"

"I had to replace the battery so it was off for a while."

"Well, that explains it. I'm looking for Charlie. Did he come over to your post?"

"Nope."

"If you do see him, tell him to give me a call okay."

"You got it."

"I'm heading over to your post now. When I get there I want an update."

"Okay."

Watkins ended his call. Kyle turned his phone off and put it in his pocket.

✱   ✱   ✱   ✱

Milo threw his camera bag down on the ground and stooped down to sit on a rock. Aerial pulled out a papaya and offered it to Milo. "No thanks. I wouldn't eat it to save my life." She put it back in her pocket and sat down beside him. They took of f their paint covered robes and threw them beside the rock they were sitting on. Milo counted the paintballs in Aerial's gun. "I'm going to keep this paintball gun for a souvenir." Aerial smiled. Milo tucked the gun under his shirt and tapped it with his hand. He smiled, guzzled some water from his bottle, and then offered it to Aerial.

"So, how much farther?" Milo asked.

"Well, we are just about there."

"Oh geeze, I'm all itchy. I think I rubbed up against some ivy." Aerial laughed at him while he started scratching all over. Milo grabbed some leaves and threw them on her. She retaliated by socking him in the face with the paint covered robes. Milo looked like a clown. Aerial laughed so hard she had to sit down for a minute to breathe.

*   *   *   *

Troy and Gibson paced around the truck. "Well, now we will have to dispose of two bodies, instead of one."

"Quiet." Troy looked through his binoculars and scanned the wooded area around him. Kyle carefully hid himself below his little rocky fort he had made until he was sure that Troy had finished looking his way.

"Troy, come here." Gibson waved him over to the trap door. "I hear Jackson on the stairs. I can't see him, but I see a small dim light way down there. Think for fun we should throw something down there and scare the crap out of him?"

Troy laughed. "That would make him madder than a hornet. Nah, I want to see him blow up in the cab!"

Gibson finished puffing on his cigarette and threw it down the hole. "Hehehe!"

Kyle carefully looked below the rocks and saw the thugs standing near some brush. He positioned his gun to line up with one of the thug's forehead. Kyle was enjoying this way too much, but knew he had orders not to do anything drastic yet. Soon, things would change quickly and he would be prepared.

*   *   *   *

Back at the lab, Dr. Collins paced around the basement as he looked at the BMW. He was still bothered by what motive a military General might have for killing the Sheriff of a small island. Dr. Collins headed upstairs to his office, shut his door, opened the cabinet under his desk and took out a small bottle of whiskey. He sat down in his chair and took out his evidence folder and began trying to slowly piece together all of the information that he had collected in the past week. He began to write down on a piece of paper each event in order from the oldest to the newest findings. After he had written an entire page, he began looking for any relationships that tied the different events to the people involved. He took a huge gulp of whiskey and rubbed his temples. Just then, someone knocked on his office door. "Come in."

Officer Garret walked into the office and said, "Watkins wanted me to give you this information about your case."

"Thanks."

Garret noticed the whisky bottle, "Drinking on the job eh? Guess I would too."

Dr. Collins smiled and waved goodbye.

After Garret had left, he opened the folder and started to read Milo Snow's testimony regarding his encounters with gunshots, military men, and a possible burglar at the local motel. He read the report a few more times, and then focused on something that had been paper clipped to the back of it. The piece of paper was titled, "**Burglary**." Underneath the title, there was a small list of items jotted down in horrible handwriting, "**a few crates, two guns, and a map found in a cabin belonging to Otis, the owner of the *Urch-***

ent Motel." The name Milo Snow was written underneath the list and the initials "ST" were at the bottom of the paper. Dr. Collins quickly picked up the phone and called Otis at the motel.

"Urchent Motel. Otis speaking."

"This is Dr. Collins. I'm calling on behalf of a case that I'm trying to solve and I have run into some information mentioning you."

"Really?"

"I found a list of things found in one of your cabins and I was wondering what the story was on it. Were you burglarized early in the week?" Otis explained everything he could remember regarding the event. "This Milo Snow guy, is he still renting a cabin from you?"

"Yes"

"Do you know when he is planning to leave the island?"

"No, sir. He is renting on a day-by-day basis."

"Okay. Will you leave a message at his cabin to have him call me immediately."

"Sure can. What is your number?"

"555-3391. Ask for Dr. Collins."

"Okay."

Dr. Collins hung up his phone and stared at his desk. He re-read the report and the list of items that Milo Snow had seen. The MAC truck and cabin had crates, so he figured that this could mean the same person involved with the truck was in the cabin. That evidence would be hard to prove, though, because the only links they had were the testimony of Milo Snow and the Sheriff's notes. Next he thought about the maps and the military officers. He remembered that Watkins had a hunch something was being smuggled. So if that was true, the maps might or might not have pointed to something.

Dr. Collins sat back on his chair and had another sip of whiskey. He made a sketchy hypothesis that the military men worked for the General who wanted to smuggle something off the island. However, he still didn't know the reasons why the General would have killed the Sheriff or what they were smuggling. The only reason he could think of for the Sheriff's murder was that he must have seen something that he wasn't supposed to and the General panicked. Maybe he saw the General and his men or overheard the General's plot? But what could the island have that was so valuable? His next idea was to call the private airport located on the north point of the island and the east ship port to find out what planes and ships were going out today and tomorrow, but first he decided to call Watkins.

*   *   *   *

Watkins was just above the ridge where he could see Kyle, when his cell phone rang. Kyle looked up as he heard the phone ringing. Gibson turned his head and told Troy to be quiet.

Watkins quickly hit the send button and ducked under a bush and whispered into the phone, "Watkins." Dr. Collins explained his sketchy conclusions and Watkins agreed with his train of thought. "Call the ports and airport immediately. I'm way too close to the truck and Kyle's post so don't call me again. The phone call almost gave my position away."

"Okay. I will wait for you to contact me."

"Later." Watkins quietly ended the call and put the phone in his pocket, switching it from ring to vibrate. He decided not to budge from the bush until he was sure he hadn't been seen. Gibson grabbed his binoculars and focused on the ridge, but didn't see Watkins under the bush. He took out his cell phone and dialed a number, "Do we have company? Get rid of it. Out." Gibson slammed the phone down and paced around the truck. Soon Jackson would be coming up from below and they were now impatiently waiting for him.

*   *   *   *

Milo looked up at the huge rocky cliff that they would have to climb. He tried not to scratch his legs and arms, even though they itched from the poison ivy he had bumped into. Milo wasn't a pro at climbing, but he liked a good challenge for himself. Aerial showed him how to grip the rocks and place his feet on the appropriately sized rocks. Milo followed her lead and they began slowly making their way up the huge rocky ridge. Finally, they made it to the top, and Aerial helped pull Milo up. They both sat down above the ridge and drank some water. Milo rubbed the sweat off of his face and arms and caught himself scratching. "How much longer until we get to the Cynna Ridge?"

"We're very close!"

Milo tried his best to look somewhat happy, but underneath his smile his muscles were aching and he really needed to find a tree to relieve himself. He wondered how Aerial could have so much energy? It almost seemed like she was a big kid, even though she was the same age as him, and he felt like a run down old man. Finally, he couldn't take the agony much longer.

"I'll be back, I need to find a large tree."

Aerial laughed, "Wow, you must have an elephant's bladder. I was sure you were going to need a tree an hour ago." Milo walked off a bit perturbed.

*   *   *   *

Watkins popped his head up and looked below him. He could see the netting above Kyle, so he carefully and quietly crept under the netting and joined Kyle. "Hey, I thought Bill would have been here."

"He is in the truck with Charlie."

"What are you talking about."

"Yeah, Charlie and Bill both got caught and locked in the back of the truck. I stayed at my post while it happened."

"Why didn't you take these two thugs out?"

"I was waiting for you."

"Okay, well I am not going to sit here all day while the guys are in the truck." Kyle paused and then said, "Tell you what, why don't you go down there and talk to the thugs. If either one of them gets feisty with you, I'll aim and shoot."

"You'd better. I'll wave my hand if I need you." Kyle nodded. Slowly, Watkins edged himself away from Kyle's post.

*   *   *   *

Milo found a huge overgrown bush behind a tree and started to relieve himself. Just behind him, he thought he heard something move and it broke his concentration. A minute later, he had calmed down, finished his business, and then headed back to where Aerial was waiting for him. Aerial jumped up from the rock she was sitting on and handed him his camera bag. "There will be some great pictures over by the ridge, so get your camera out."

Milo retrieved his camera and took an extra moment to switch to his telephoto lense. A short while later, they had made it to their destination and Milo started taking pictures of the Cynna Ridge. "We're here!" Aerial said. "Now look down and check out the land-scape. Isn't it beautiful?" Just as Milo did, he saw Watkins slinking down the bank below him, a huge MAC truck, and two very unhappy thugs with guns. Milo gulped, "Beautiful can't describe it."

CHAPTER 11

▼

Watkins hid behind the front of the truck. He knew he could only take one of the men at a time, so he waved for Kyle to stun one of them with a bullet. Watkins pulled his rifle around him and loaded it. He watched the thugs walking around him. When Gibson was alone, he yelled, "You there, put down your machine gun. You and your pal are under arrest for the murder of Detective Richardson." Gibson froze but did not put down his gun. Gibson retracted his gun and waved to Troy. Watkins yelled again, "Don't move. I want you both to turn around with your hands up. Guns on the ground now!" Watkins waved to Kyle and he got ready. Gibson and Troy laid their guns down and then turned away from him, putting their hands up. As Watkins approached them, Gibson and Troy spun around and started to grab Watkins. Kyle had lined up his gun with Troy's chest and shot off two rounds. Troy fell flat on his face, while Gibson punched Watkins in the stomach. Watkins fell down and fired off one round into Gibson's thigh. Gibson fell down and screamed like a baby. Watkins grabbed Gibson's hands and hand-cuffed them together. At the same time, he had passed out from the

shock of the wound to his thigh and never felt Watkins tie a handkerchief around it to control the bleeding.

Above the chaos, Milo grabbed Aerial and showed her what was
going on below them. Just then, Milo noticed out of the side of his
eye something moving under a rocky brush area. He picked up his
power zoom lense and focused in on the brush. All he could make
out was black netting around the rocks and then he saw a foot. Milo
gulped and whispered to Aerial what he saw.

"Milo, take a few pictures just in case."

Milo nodded and began taking picture after picture of the events
happening below them.

In a flash, Watkins ran over to the back of the truck. Just as he
started to pull the latch on the door, he heard a noise behind him
and spun around. The brush above the trap door started to move as
Jackson yelled loudly, "Help me with this gold you droits." Watkins
stood staring at him. Jackson was blinded by the light and shielded
his eyes. After his vision came back in focus, he saw both his bodyguards lying on the ground. "What the hell is going on up here?"
Jackson grabbed his gun. "Wake up you idiots." Neither of them
moved.

Watkins looked at Jackson, pulled out his gun, and said, "So, are
you the General that killed my Sheriff?"

Jackson turned his head in his direction. "Yeah, I killed your
Sheriff. He got in my way."

"You are under arrest. Drop your gun and put your hands behind
your back."

"I will not." Jackson lifted his gun and pointed it at Watkins. The two men stood face to face with guns pointing at their chests.

Milo ran out of film and stepped away from the ledge. He carefully put his camera back in his backpack and watched as Aerial began to sob quietly.

Aerial whispered, "He was my godfather." Milo comforted her, until she calmed down. Now Milo understood the relationship. Aerial's first reaction was to help Watkins and kill Jackson herself, but to her surprise, something else unexpected happened. Just as she started to move, she saw someone get up from under the netting and run down the bank. Aerial realized who it was and stood still. Kyle ran over to where Jackson was standing and pointed a gun in his face.

"Who the hell are you?" Jackson yelled.

"The General's apprentice."

Jackson shouted, "I am cursed!" as he remembered the inscribed words written on the treasure chest. Just then, Kyle shot him between his eyes, and his body dropped to the ground.

Watkins was appalled. "Nice backup, but you didn't need to go that far. I could have handled him."

"Sorry, I only take orders from the General and he was mine."

"You mean, that wasn't the General?" Kyle just smiled and walked past Watkins.

Aerial saw Kyle collecting huge bags and pacing around Watkins. "Milo, we have to help him. Kyle is going to kill Watkins! My godfather often said he couldn't be trusted and that he was very money hungry."

Milo tried to think how he could help without getting himself killed. Nothing was coming to mind.

"I think that is Kyle's sniper post. I'll go under there and see if I can't line him up, if you go and distract him." Aerial said.

Milo gave her a frozen deer-in-the-headlights look and started to hyperventilate. "Are you kidding me?"

Aerial replied, "You can do it and I can be awfully grateful!" Milo scratched his leg and thought about it for a second. Aerial had been quite convincing, so he hid his backpack underneath some rocks and ran down the bank quietly. Milo was sweating like a pig. He felt like he was in a pressure cooker. 'What next?' he thought as he wiped the sweat from his bangs. He looked for a hiding place and ran over to the front of the truck.

Kyle raised the back door of the truck. Bill saw it was Kyle and put down his gun and started to walk toward the door. All of the sudden, Kyle swung his gun toward Bill, fired off a shot, and Bill dropped like a rock out of the back off the truck.

"Kyle!" Watkins shouted.

He looked at Watkins and pointed his gun at him, "Get into the truck."

"Don't think so, Kyle." Kyle cocked his gun and repeated his request as he threw Watkin's rifle aside.

Milo didn't know what to do, until he suddenly remembered a movie he had once seen with a private eye running out to save his partner. So, he grabbed his paint gun under his shirt and pointed it to Kyle's back. "Don't move, or I'll shoot." Kyle stopped and dropped his gun to his side. Meanwhile, Aerial lined up the gun barrel to Kyle's back. Milo had him slowly turn around.

Kyle stared at Milo's gun as it was facing him head on and noticed a speck of blue at the end of the barrel. Kyle smiled and grabbed for Milo just as Aerial squeezed off a shot, which hit him in the shoulder. He flew to the ground, but quickly grabbed Milo's leg and brought him down with him. Kyle's gun had landed out of reach, but his army knife had fallen out of it's sheath, landing next to them. They both rolled around trying to get the knife. Aerial lined up another shot, but missed horribly. Milo felt metal, and grabbed. A gun! He brought it up and squeezed the trigger. A green paintball slammed into Kyle's chest.

Milo cursed, "Wrong gun." Of course, from point blank range, even a paintball stings, so Milo had half-of-a-second to go back to scrambling with Kyle for the knife. Just then, Watkins ran over. He grabbed his backup gun from his ankle and pointed it at Milo and Kyle.

"Get up NOW! Milo move away." Too late. Kyle had reached his army knife and then grabbed Milo across the neck. Aerial panicked. She couldn't hit Kyle because now Milo was in front of him, so she quickly racked her brain for ideas. Watkins paced around Kyle. "Let Milo go."

"No way. Drop the gun or he gets it." Aerial reached in her pocket and found the papaya. She had been a great pitcher when she was younger so she decided to wing a fast ball at Kyle's head. as a distraction. Watkins was keeping his gun on Kyle when the pear shaped fruit came flying down from the bank and knocked Kyle in the head causing him to drop his knife as he grabbed for his new bruise. Milo was still pulling loose from his other arm as Watkins put a bullet in Kyle's chest. His body fell backwards and his blood splattered all over Milo's white polo shirt. The papaya rolled over to

Milo's foot and he picked it up as he got up. Remembering what he had said before about not eating it unless it saved his life, he took a big bite.

Watkins looked at Milo, "Nice war paint."

Aerial came running down the bank, screaming, "My knight!" and gave Milo a big hug and a kiss.

Inside the truck, Charlie slowly pulled the plastic tarp away from himself and crawled out of the truck. That ended up scaring the daylights out of Milo, who spun around and plugged him with a paintball.

"It's okay. I'm a good guy." Milo nearly had a heart attack.

"Bill, you okay?" Charlie asked. Bill groaned, and slowly sat upright.

"My head is killing me. Lucky for me I have a hard head and the bullet just nicked me." Charlie laughed and Milo started to breathe again, his hands still shaking as he realized he had just shot another person.

Watkins looked at Milo and said, "Good reaction time. You sure you aren't undercover?" Milo frowned.

Watkins decided what to do with Gibson. He figured tying him up in the cab of the truck would be a good place for him. Gibson was still unconscious from the wound, so Watkins uncuffed one of his hands so when he did snap out of it, he could hold the handkerchief on his thigh to help control the bleeding. 'Rotten thug,' Watkins thought, as he closed the door to the cab. Next, he debated what he should do with the bodies because it would be a while before the crime team would be there. He figured it was not good for tourists to catch a glimpse of this from the trail above, so he carefully placed the bodies and gold in the back of the truck. As he laid

Jackson on the floor of the truck, a piece of folded up paper fell out of his pocket. Watkins, who was never one to let evidence get away, picked it up and stuffed it in his pocket to save for later. He closed and latched the door, then grabbed his cell phone, and called the station to send more police officers to the scene. He reminded himself he was going to have to add some new boys to his force after this mess was filed and dismissed. After that he walked over to Milo and extended his hand for a good hand shake.

"What a day. You do realize that you saved my life. I would love to know how you did it?"

Milo smiled. "I think I've seen one too many movies."

Watkins smiled and laughed. "I wouldn't put it past you. The green paintball was real classy! Hehehe." Just then, Bill began to feel dizzy and passed out on the ground, accidentally knocking Milo over.

Acrial ran over to Bill and took his pulse. "He must have a concussion. He's not doing well. We need to get him help fast." Milo stood up and rubbed the leaves off his legs as he watched Watkins pick up his phone and called the hospital emergency line. He gave their position and asked for the chopper.

✳   ✳   ✳   ✳

At the lab, Dr. Collins had made a lot of progress. He had called the airport, the shipping dock, and got the list of the boats and private planes that were taking off that evening. He started to make a list of the names when his phone rang.

"Yes."

"Hi, Clyde. Just wanted to let you know you can cancel your phone calls to the airport and dock. Remember my hunch?"

"Yeah"

"Well, we have two dead men, two wounded men, a missing General, who may also possibly be dead, and a lot of gold coins."

"We better send the team out to investigate the bodies. What about the military men?"

"We haven't seen them. They might still be around somewhere. There is a huge hole leading down to something underground. I'm going to investigate. Can you get out here immediately?"

"We are on our way." Dr. Collins hung his phone up and ran out of his office. He gave out the new orders and soon everyone was piling into the van.

*   *   *   *

Charlie poked his foot around the hole that Jackson had come up from. Watkins walked over toward him and looked down the entrance way. "Geeze, look at those steep stairs. They must go down for at least a mile."

Watkins rubbed his head. "Something doesn't add up. If the General killed the Sheriff, then this should be the guy that came up from below. But, according to Kyle, he wasn't the General. So where is the General? And who is this guy?" Charlie pointed down the hole. Watkins paced around, "You up for an expedition?"

"Wish we had a map."

"Oh! Hang on a second." Watkins took the paper out of his pocket and unfolded it to see what it was. "Charlie, look at this." Watkins laid out the map and showed Charlie.

"Woah! This is a serious treasure map, eh?" They both studied the map and looked at each other.

"This is a really old map. Look at the date on this."

"So, there is a long staircase to a door that opens if you solve this riddle."

"Okay. Then what?"

"Looks like once you go in, you then have to push these huge stones to open the secret tomb."

"Weird!"

"You don't think the General is still down there or escaped through another chamber not shown on the map?"

"I have no idea, but the gold is here, so I doubt there will be anyone else coming up now."

Just then Charlie had an idea. "Hold that thought." He heard groaning coming from the cab, so he walked over to the cab and started to talk to Gibson. "Is your General down below? Who is the guy that came up with the coins?" Gibson rolled his eyes. "Look, you are the only witness left, and we need answers." As Charlie walked away from the cab and back over to Watkins, Gibson noticed a key sticking out of the ignition. "He won't talk. Looks like it's just you and me and the big black hole!"

Watkins told Milo and Aerial their plan and that they should stay with Bill and ride back to town on the chopper. They agreed, and watched the men slowly start down the hole. Just as their heads reached ground level, they heard the sound of the ignition starting in the truck. Gibson had chosen death over a jail sentence. A split second later, as they turned to run back up, the cab blew to pieces. Milo and Aerial fell to the ground as truck parts rained upon them. Watkins popped his head up. "Dammit! There goes our witness."

Milo rolled and looked at Aerial, asking, "Are you okay?"

"Only if the surprises stop." They stayed with Bill until the rescue chopper came.

Arriving on the scene, the EMT ran over to Milo and grabbed his wrist and asked him to lie down quickly.

"You're bleeding."

"No, it's not my blood." Milo pointed to Bill. "This guy needs help. Not me."

The EMT looked relieved. Aerial helped the EMT put Bill on the stretcher and asked if she and Milo could go to the hospital with him. The EMT granted them chopper privileges, even though there was hardly any space for them to fit. Soon the helicopter headed away from the scene and headed back to the small town. The chopper was loud, and there weren't enough headsets to go around, so Milo grabbed his hanky and tried to stuff some in each ear, which left the hanky draped across his face. Aerial couldn't resist the image of Milo at that moment, so she leaned over and yelled in his ear, "My masked hero!" and then promptly fell asleep on his shoulder. Milo sighed.

Charlie and Watkins slowly proceeded down the steep stairs, both wishing this day would soon end. They used Jackson's lantern to guide their way. Watkins said, "Can you believe this guy walked up all these stairs with those heavy bundles of gold coins?"

"Unbelievable. I'm not looking forward to carrying myself up!"

"Don't you think it seems odd for one person to carry so much?"

"Yeah. Wonder where those other military men are?"

"I really hope they're not down here and armed."

"Me too."

Watkins then stopped and thought about the situation. "Charlie, we need to go back up. This is too dangerous for just you and me. Lots of people have died over the last few days. Let's just wait until we have more officers. I have a bad feeling about this, and besides, I can always call for the national guard team to come and check this out."

"That sounds good. Especially the part about making someone else do the stairs." They both turned around and headed back up from below.

*   *   *   *

A while later, the chopper dropped Milo and Aerial at the hospital with Bill, and they stayed there until Bill regained consciousness. Aerial asked to use a phone, and called Watkins to let him know Bill's status.

A nurse applied some calamine lotion to Milo's legs and arms and told him no scratching. He went into the small bathroom and looked at himself in the mirror. Aerial was right, he did look like a streaked clown. He found a washcloth and ran some water on it to gently remove the paint from his face. Milo wasn't sure what he wanted to do next, but he knew he either wanted to take a hot shower or fall asleep for two days. Hmmm. Maybe both. He walked out of the bathroom and talked to Bill until Aerial returned. A short while later, Aerial came in with some food for Bill and said goodbye.

"Watkins will probably see you tomorrow. Get some rest."

Bill waved and said, "You two love birds be good."

Milo grabbed Aerial and they walked out of the room, down the hallway, and out into the fresh air. "What next, Milo?"

"Bed, bath, food. Not in that order! I'm exhausted."

"Ok. Dinner and then bed." They walked the short distance to the restaurant to get some dinner. Just then Milo remembered something and shouted, "Doggone it!"

Aerial looked surprised. "What's wrong?"

"I left my backpack under some rocks and I forgot to get it."

Aerial rubbed his shoulder and said, "No problem. The team will be out there all night. I will call Watkins and let him know to bring it back to the station."

Milo grumbled.

*   *   *   *

Dr. Collins and his team arrived at the north point of the island. He pulled out his cell phone and called Watkins to find out where they were. Watkins unfolded the map and said, "According to this paper, there is a hidden turn-off two point two miles south of the hiking trail. There is a penciled note that says, "**Look for a grove of bamboo and make a hard right**." You should be able to see tire tracks from that point on."

"Okay. See you soon." Dr. Collins replied.

*   *   *   *

At the ridge, Charlie grabbed his pack that had been thrown over behind a thick area of bushes and noticed the beginnings of a terrible odor. He waved toward Watkins and pointed behind the bushes, mouthing the word, "Body." Watkins ran down the bank and over to Charlie. They dug around the bushes and found a hat with five gold stars. Charlie bent over the body and said, "Pleasure to meet you, General."

CHAPTER 12

▼

Milo and Aerial arrived at the restaurant, which was just about to close. They walked in, waved to a waitress, and sat themselves at a booth. "Just think. This day began right here."

"Wish I felt as good as I did hours ago, before I got the itchy rash from the poison ivy, the aching muscles from rock climbing, and my neck being out of joint from fighting with someone." Aerial couldn't help laughing at him. They ordered their dinners and slowly savored each bite. After they finished their clams and crabs, Milo dropped his head on the table and started to snore.

Aerial got up from the table, made a phone call to Watkins about Milo's backpack, and then grabbed one of her friends. "This is a Kodak moment. Do you have a camera?"

"In my purse. It's a disposable but it'll work."

"Okay." Aerial shot a few pictures of him sleeping on the table. "Wish it had a microphone. He is louder than a saw!"

The women giggled and thought it was kind of cute. "Should we put a blanket around him and just let him sleep here?"

"Yep." Aerial removed the plates and silverware from the table and locked the restaurant door. The wait staff cleaned the dining room and the kitchen. A while later, everyone had left except for Aerial and Milo. She pulled up a bench, laid her head beside Milo, and closed her eyes.

*   *   *   *

A while later, Dr. Collins and the team finally arrived at the bottom of the ridge. They got out and started to bag the bodies and clean up the mess. Dr. Collins sat beside Watkins on a rock who was playing with the straps of a bright blue backpack. "Hell of a day."

"You're telling me. I have quite a story to share with you."

"I bet!"

"I'm exhausted. I'm heading home and I'll see you for breakfast. Think I can bum a ride from one of you?"

"Sure, I'll make sure that Garret drops you off." A while later, the team had finished what they could before dark and Dr. Collins motioned them back to the van.

Watkins had arrived at the police station and walked into his office. He sat at his desk and checked his messages. Nothing looked too eye catching, so he turned off his desk light and headed home. On his way, he left a message on Dr. Atkin's answering machine to meet him for breakfast at the *Happy Clams* restaurant around 7 a.m. His cell phone beeped "Low battery," and he knew that wasn't the only thing he needed to recharge.

*   *   *   *

The next morning dawned bright and clear. Aerial woke up from the noise she heard coming from the kitchen. She nudged Milo and he sat straight up. Milo looked puzzled, "Please tell me I didn't sleep here all night. But my really sore neck tells me I did. I think?"

Aerial smiled at him and nodded. "Are you hungry?"

"Coffee would be great! The parts of my body that don't hurt are itching like crazy. Do you have any calamine lotion?"

"Not with me. But we'll fix you up later."

Milo rubbed the crusties out of his eyes and yawned. Just then, he saw Watkins and Dr. Collins pass the restaurant window and groaned.

Aerial was supposed to work the morning shift anyhow, so she put on her apron, and unlocked the front door. Watkins and Dr. Collins walked in and Aerial sat them at a table. Milo waved them over, and Watkins said, "Man, I thought you looked bad yesterday, but at least your war paint is gone."

"Yeah, well, I had hoped to start at least one of my days without bumping into the police. This is clearly not my week."

"Well, at least you aren't on my crap list!" Watkins replied. Milo brightened a bit at that.

"Sit down and give me a break. I haven't had my coffee yet."

"Here, I think this belongs to you." Milo grabbed his backpack and said, "Thanks!" as he quickly rummaged through it to make sure his camera and gear was not damaged. Aerial brought them menus, and they ordered eggs and bacon. Milo listened to the entire story that Watkins shared with Dr. Collins regarding the ancient treasure and the General's plot to steal it. Unfortunately, Milo's really strong hints that he should get some of the gold fell on deaf ears. Instead, Watkins insisted that the gold would probably have to be shipped back to Spain, from what he could tell so far, and if not, the police force could use some new cars and helicopters. Milo ate a piece of bacon in disgust. After Watkins and Dr. Collins had finished their breakfast, they paid their bill, and went their separate ways.

Milo motioned for Aerial to come over to the table. As she cleared the dishes from the table, he asked her for a ride out to the north point of the island to pick up his car after her shift was over. She responded, "No problem. See you sometime after 1 p.m." Milo said, "Good. I would like a little bit more time with you before my flight leaves, so this will give us a chance to spend the afternoon together."

"You're leaving?" It came out a bit flat, and more than a little cold.

"Yeah. I am booked on the red-eye tonight. My boss is getting anxious for my pictures and he is not going to like my bill from my stay here. This, as you can see, was no vacation."

Aerial thawed a bit and replied the words "Later gator," to him, but he knew she was upset. He paid his bill, grabbed his backpack, and left the restaurant.

Milo walked as slow as a snail back to his cabin. Every muscle and bone ached in his body, so the first thing he was going to do was take a hot shower for about a half an hour at least. He even admitted to himself that, 'Good plumbers are worth the money!' After his shower, he dried himself off and put on a fresh set of clothes. He saw the blue backpack sitting on the chair and remembered that he needed to develop the film so that Watkins had some proof of what went on the day before. As he waited for the developer to work, he packed his bags and cleaned up his room. The pictures all turned out well and he loved the ones he had taken of Aerial. He grabbed a manila folder and marked it, "**For Watkins**." He sorted the pictures and kept what he wanted and then organized the pictures into the folder. He stared out the window and looked at the cabin beside him. He got a chill looking at it, rubbed his head where his stitches were, then closed the folder addressed to Watkins, and placed it in his bag. Milo pondered the idea of writing a book about this trip, 'But who would believe it?' he thought, as he grabbed his other manila folder, labeled "**Island Pictures.**" He opened it, took out the two pictures that Aerial liked, put them aside for safe keeping, and then placed the remaining sorted pictures into it. After he finished packing everything up he put his luggage and camera bags on the front porch. He checked his watch and decided to make a quick trip to the small souvenir shop. Milo walked over to the shop and purchased two picture frames, some postcards, one newspaper, some scotch tape, a bottle of calamine lotion, and an urchin seashell. Aerial was going to be picking him up very soon, so he walked as fast as he could without too much pain and got back to his cabin. He waited a few minutes and then saw Aerial pulling up to his cabin. He came outside and greeted her. She piled his luggage and camera bags in the back of her jeep and waited for him while he turned in his key to the manager. Otis greeted him and asked him what happened the day before and explained about the phone call from Dr. Collins. In return, Milo gave him a brief summary and kept it short and sweet.

"So was the guy in my cabin one of the thugs that was involved?"

"Yep. I recognized him, but this time he had been knocked out!"

"Well, as they say, what goes around comes around!" Milo laughed. "Come back anytime Mr. Snow. We will be anxious to see your write up!"

"Me too!" Milo replied, as he signed his paperwork. He waved goodbye to Otis and his wife, who passed him as he was walking out of the office, and headed outside to the parking lot. As he approached Aerial, he handed her something wrapped in newspaper.

"Open it after I leave, okay?"

"Sure will!" Aerial drove Milo to the north point of the island to pick up his rental car.

Milo got his car and followed Aerial back to town. She had him follow her to her beach house. He parked his car and met up with her on foot.

"Hungry?"

"Yes."

"How about if I make us some sandwiches."

"Sounds good! As long as they aren't peanut butter!" Milo relaxed on the porch looking out over the ocean. This was the first time he could actually sit down and enjoy watching the waves crash into the shore. Aerial brought out tuna sandwiches and two sodas. They ate their sandwiches together and talked about different things.

For the remaining part of the day, they grabbed a blanket and sat out on the beach. Milo was in dire need of a tan where his shirt had covered, so Aerial made sure he got some good sun rays on his pale white skin. A while later, they played in the waves and splashed water on each other. They had a great day together and ended up enjoying each other so much that they forgot that Milo was leaving in a matter of hours. Aerial made a late dinner for Milo and explained a bit more in detail about her relationship with her godfather.

"Years ago, the Sheriff was best friends with my Dad. When I was baptized, my parents decided to ask him if he would like to be my godfather. He accepted and was almost like a second father to me. Last year, he was with me at my Dad's funeral and kept his protective wings close by me. My parents had separated when I was a teenager, so my Dad did the best he could with me. The rest of the time, I spent with the Thompson's family. But, now that he has died, I am not sure what I plan to do on the island from this point on. I know I already miss him as badly as my father." She paused for a moment, wiped the corner of her eye, and then asked, "Any suggestions?"

Milo gulped. "Well, I know I can't offer you too much, but I would really enjoy having you come with me to New York, so we could maybe start a new life together. I'm crazy about you, Aerial, and I would hate to lose you. So, if it's not too much to ask, would you fly home with me?" Milo paused as he waited for a negative answer to surface.

Aerial became quiet for more than a few seconds, before she looked at him and said, "I was hoping you would ask me." Milo breathed a sigh of relief, grabbed Aerial, and gave her a long kiss.

After she cleared the table, she walked him to his car.

"I have a few phone calls to make and some major packing to do, but I will meet you at the airport for the flight tonight."

Milo beamed all over as he started his engine. Aerial waved as he pulled out of her driveway and as he looked back in his rearview mirror, he watched her mouth the words, "I love you!" He honked his horn in response and sped down the road.

On his way to the airport, he made one last stop at the police station. He walked in and asked to see Watkins. Officer Garret gestured to him and then followed him back to his office.

"Mr. Snow here to see you, sir." Milo walked in as Officer Garret departed. Watkins smiled and offered him a hand shake.

Milo shook his hand and said, "Just a little something for you to remember me by."

He laid the manila folder on his desk and waved goodbye. Just as he was making his smooth exit, he tripped over the door jam and fell backwards into a trash can. Watkins howled! He hadn't laughed that hard in days. He ran over to Milo and helped him up as he brushed coffee grinds and cigarette butts off of his head, "Good job twinkle toes!"

Milo groaned, "Why me?"

His final stop was to drop his car off at the crummy rental place. He drove it into the parking lot, grabbed his luggage, and handed the keys back to the lady standing at the counter. The shuttle bus was waiting outside the car rental place, so he found a seat and piled his stuff beside him. A little while later, the shuttle bus had picked up enough people for it to head to the airport. He arrived at the main gate, got out his ticket, gave his luggage to the clerk, and walked over to the waiting area for the gate. He found Aerial and gave her a hug. Just then, their flight was called. "Any problems buying a ticket?"

Aerial responded, "It helps to have friends in high places!" Milo smiled as he rummaged through his pocket for his ticket. He handed it to the lady and boarded the small plane, with Aerial beside him.

It was going to be a really, really long flight home. He found a pillow and stuffed it under his head and tried to relax until the plane would begin to take off. As the passengers finished piling into the plane, he reached down and opened his cell phone, noticing he had one message. He had a bad feeling about it, but figured he had better check it just in case. Milo hit his send button and listened to the message. All of a sudden, Milo could feel his blood pressure rising as he heard the word, "Swanson," and he shouted out loud, "Your sending me where?" The stewardess ran over to Milo and tried to calm him down, but it was too late, the airline pillow had been torn into pieces. Aerial giggled and whispered into Milo's ear, "I think my vacation has just started!"

THE END

0-595-29585-1

CPSIA information can be obtained
at www.ICGtesting.com
Printed in the USA
BVOW08s0356200317
478794BV00001B/3/P

9 780595 295852